Bitches and Brawlers

THE RED CAPE SOCIETY, BOOK 4

MELANIE KARSAK

CLOCKPUNK PRESS

BITCHES AND BRAWLERS
A Red Riding Hood Retelling
The Red Cape Society, Book 4
Copyright © 2018 Clockpunk Press
All rights reserved. No part of this book may be used or reproduced without permission from the author.
This is a work of fiction. References to historical people, organizations, events, places, and establishments are the product of the author's imagination or are used fictitiously. Any resemblance to living persons is purely coincidental.
Editing by Becky Stephens Editing
Proofreading by Siren Editing
Cover art by Art by Karri

❦ Created with Vellum

In loving memory of Helen Morrison

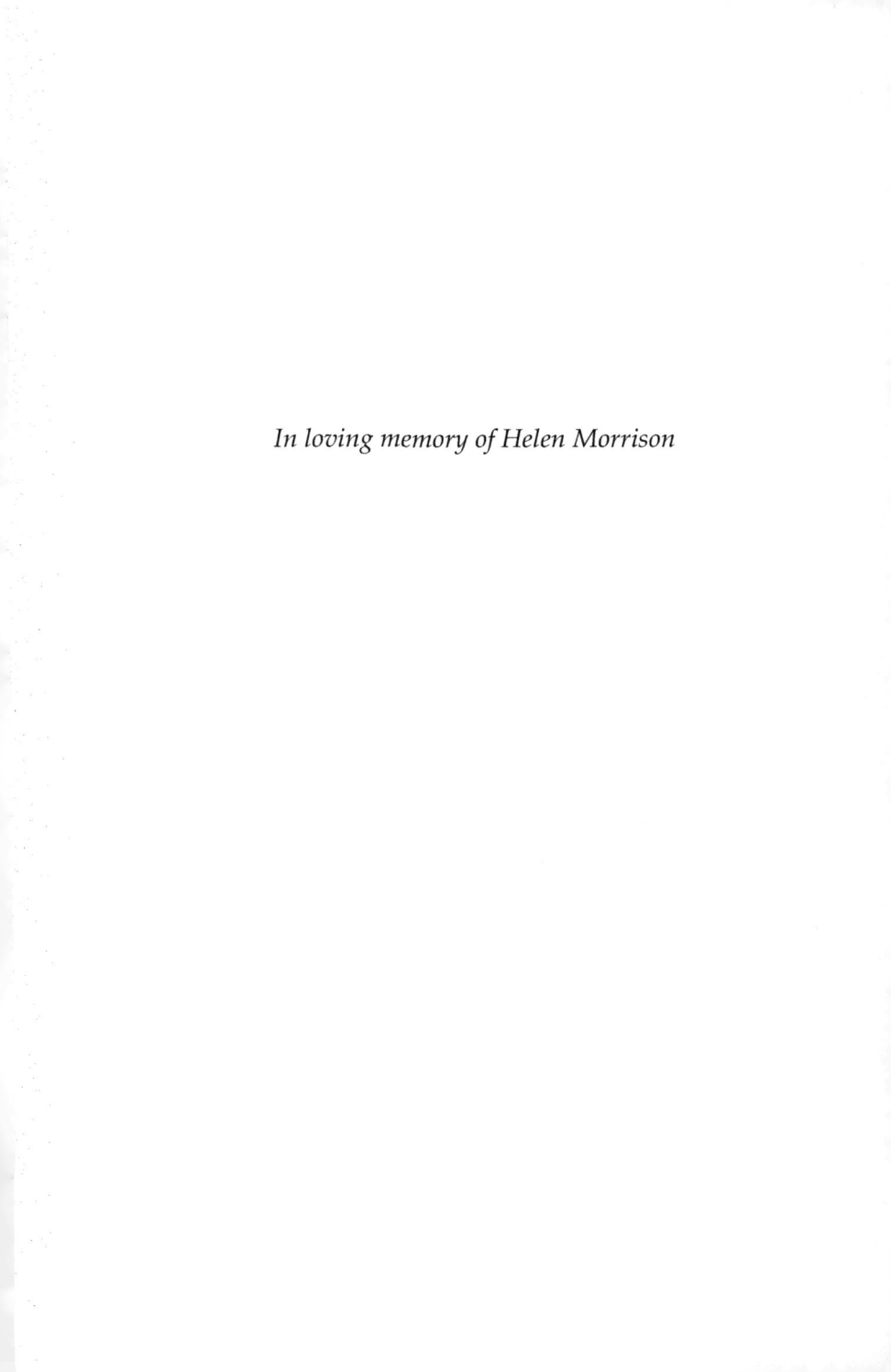

Bitches and Brawlers

CHAPTER 1
Sneaky is as Sneaky Does

I rubbed my hands together and blew warm air onto my fingers. The long winter had lingered into spring. And I had spent entirely too much time on rooftops waiting for bad people to do bad things.

"Well, one good thing about my beat, I don't have to wait around in the cold all night long," Agent Keung whispered.

I smirked. "No, I suppose the opium dens are rather warm. Don't you get a headache though?"

Agent Keung grinned. "Only the good kind. Have you ever partaken, Agent Louvel?"

"No. I have quite enough vices. Mine are mostly of the sugar and butter variety, though."

He chuckled. "I spend far more time in opium dens and brothels than I need or want."

"You see, the clean, crisp air will do you some good."

"If it's all the same to you, I'd prefer to never work your beat ever again."

I chuckled. "Well, then let's see what we can do about your missing shaman."

Agent Keung nodded. "All of Limehouse is in an uproar," he said, referring to the small, east end Chinese community. While many good families lived there, the place was polluted by brothels and opium houses. Located near the river, it was a popular spot for sailors and others who had picked up the opium habit. "They believe the entire opium market will fall apart without Master Qiang controlling the spirits that watch over it."

I looked back at him over my shoulder. "One of my fluffy friends is interested in your shaman for a reason. *Does* he control spirits?"

Agent Keung nodded. "Yes, but it's not the spirits watching over the opium dens I'm worried about. It's the other creatures Master Qiang controls that we must keep at bay."

"Lovely. Of what variety?"

"Elementals. Harmless when controlled. Dangerous as demons when they aren't. Not the type we want roaming about the realm."

"Why can't they ever lord over something quaint? Garden gnomes would be a nice change of pace."

Agent Keung chuckled. "In theory. But I can't imagine taking on a horde of possessed garden gnomes. Can you?"

I grinned, the image of hundreds of inches-high men in red hats on the attack. "You paint quite the picture."

"Spirits are no fun to tangle with, but I have to say, I don't care much for your pets, Agent Louvel. Not a very civilized bunch."

"They aren't all bad," I replied, my mind drifting to Lionheart. I was surprised when I felt my heartbeat quicken a little at the thought of his wolfy grin. "Just don't get too cozy with them on a full moon."

Agent Keung chuckled lightly.

While the Templars were civil, there had been more and more disruptions with other rogue wolves over the last few months. The Dís was right. They were testing Lionheart's reign. Mostly it had been small fires to stamp out, but the tingling of my palms told me something big was on the horizon. Lionheart was getting tight-lipped and hard to track down. Was he avoiding me? Why would he do that? The issue vexed me to no end. I had a feeling something was happening just under my nose. The last time the werewolves started swiping other preternaturals, Agent Reid had died, and Quinn had almost been killed. Now? I just didn't know what was going on.

It was only when Agent Keung spotted the werewolves in Limehouse that pieces of the puzzle started to slowly fall together.

"There," Agent Keung whispered, jerking his chin in the direction of an auto creeping slowly down the street toward the building on the opposite block.

We were lingering on the edge of a dark district. Whatever someone was up to, they didn't want to be seen. Which meant we were in the right spot.

The auto's lights extinguished, the purr of the boiler and the soft hiss of steam the only indication that the vehicle was coming. The auto rolled to a stop outside a dilapidated building.

Hidden in the shadows, Agent Keung and I watched. The driver, a heavily muscled brute of a werewolf, stepped out. I recognized him as one of Fenton's old pack members. He was the third I'd seen this week of the old group. They'd started returning from Australia. Why? Surely, they knew they weren't going to get a second chance to stay away. And why wasn't Lionheart or the Templars doing something to stop them?

The driver opened the door of the auto.

A pair of long, shapely legs emerged first. Fenton's old dog reached to help the passenger out.

Hell's bells. Alodie. As always, she was dressed beautifully. In a silver silk gown, her pale blond hair perfectly arranged under a black mini top hat, she scanned the street then turned and headed toward the building. I should have known. If something unsavory and sneaky was happening, naturally she would be involved.

Two more female werewolves emerged from the auto. I recognized the Lolitas from the brothel, but they were sporting entirely different attire these days. Dressed in trousers, boots, and corsets, both of them were armed. They eyed the street, their eyes flashing red.

I heard the sound of struggle as one of the Lolitas pulled a man out of the car. An older man with long white hair dressed in long robes stumbled as he stepped out, tripping over the curb. They'd put a bag over his head and bound his hands behind his back. One of the Lolita girls grabbed him roughly, tugging him to his feet.

"That's him," Agent Keung whispered.

"Why doesn't he just roast their rotten hides?" I whispered.

"Look at his binds."

I increased the magnification on my optic and scanned down to see the glint of something green around the shaman's wrists.

"Jade," Agent Keung explained. "That will hold him. But your werewolves really are stupid. If he ever gets free…"

"Would serve them right. They *are* stupid and predictable, for the most part. But that bitch," I whispered, gesturing to Alodie, "is trouble."

Two werewolves appeared from the basement entrance below the building. Alodie gestured to the shaman. One of the wolves grabbed Master Qiang and pulled him toward the door.

The Lolitas scanned the street once more then turned and followed Alodie inside.

I sighed. "Complications. Always complications." I slipped my gun back into my holster then eyed the rooftop. I motioned to Agent Keung, and we raced to the other side of the building. We slipped down the ladder into the alley opposite the structure where Alodie and the others had gone. Staying in the shadows, we worked our way to the end of the alley.

I pulled my silver blade and eyed the building. The driver was guarding the car, and there was another werewolf at the door. I looked back at Agent Keung. "If you want your shaman, we're going to need to go in to get him. It's probably going to get messy."

Agent Keung reached behind his back where he wore a sword. The blade seemed to sing as it came out of its scabbard, the metal glinting in the moonlight.

"Agent Hunter told me to come prepared. The blade is forged with silver. Thought it might come in handy."

I grinned at the mention of Edwin's name, my heart fluttering for just a moment.

"Nice," I replied. Moving quickly, we headed across the street. I motioned to Agent Keung to go for the driver while I went after the guard. Swift and silent, Keung was on top of the driver before the werewolf spotted him. A moment later, the two were fighting. Keung whacked the gun from the werewolf's hand and roundhouse kicked the wolf who tried to lunge at him, knocking the werewolf off his feet.

Distracted by the sound of the fight, the guard moved away from the door. Hidden near the stairs, I moved quickly to intercept him.

Catching a glimpse of me out of the corner of his eye, the werewolf turned and faced me. I recognized him as one of the former members of Paddington Pack.

"Little Red," he said with a growl. At once, he began to shift form. His human features contorted, his mouth elongating, his teeth forming sharp rows in his snout-like mouth. His eyes flashed red.

Taking aim, I lobbed my dagger at him just as he lunged.

My dagger worked faster than his muscles. The silver blade slammed into his chest. The impact knocked him off his feet. His howl died in his throat as he dropped to the ground.

I turned in time to watch Keung's blade slide

through the air, taking the driver's head with it. It bounced across the street toward me.

I knelt and studied the face. Definitely one of Fenton's old boys. Frowning, I went and retrieved my dagger from the Paddington wolf.

Agent Keung joined me.

"You need to teach me some of those moves," I told Agent Keung.

"Come by my kwoon for some sparring. Not that you need it, *Little Red*."

I smirked at him then turned and looked at the door. All right, Alodie. What are you up to?

CHAPTER 2
Test Your Might

Moving slowly, Keung and I went to the door. My pistol drawn, I opened the door. It was pitch black. Activating my night optic, the hallway before me came into focus, tinted in shades of green. I motioned to Keung, and we headed inside.

There was the distinct scent of werewolves in the air, but more than that, it was she-wolves I smelled. That strange, musky feminine odor permeated everything. I swallowed hard, the scent gag-worthy.

Somewhere inside, I heard a shrill voice followed by the soft sound of Master Qiang cursing the wolves in Chinese.

I looked back at Keung. He nodded, having heard as well.

I frowned and tried to reach out with my senses. There would be four wolves in total: two bitches, a guard, and Alodie. She might look pretty, but I had to remember that Alodie was a beta. I pulled my other pistol from my boot as we moved toward the room at the end of the hallway. The light of an oil lamp therein cast an orange glow.

"No need to be so disagreeable, Master Qiang. All I need is a little confirmation. Once you provide that, you can take your granddaughter and go," Alodie purred.

I looked back at Keung who shook his head in surprise.

We crept slowly toward the room.

Inside, there was a tense silence.

A moment later, I heard the distinct sound of a slap.

A girl cried out in pain. "Grandfather," she called in a tearful whisper.

My teeth ground together, and it was all I could do to stop myself from barging into the room and murdering everyone. But I needed to know what was happening. What was Alodie doing?

"Stop," Master Qiang shouted.

"The map, Master Qiang," Alodie said.

"Unbind me," the old man said.

"No, Alodie. He'll turn on us," one of the Lolitas said.

"You stupid wolf, I can't do what you're asking with my hands bound. Unbind me."

"Very well," Alodie said. "No tricks, or we'll eat her for supper. Understood?"

"I hear you."

There was some movement in the room. I heard the rattle of paper and the sound of a chair scraping on the floor.

"Where was his last known location?" the shaman asked.

"We sent someone to the American southwest to retrieve him. I need to know where they are now," Alodie said.

"Give me the bone," Master Qiang said.

I heard the sound of a box opening. A moment later, Master Qiang began chanting. The light from the lamp within flickered then went out. All at once, it grew terribly cold. Goosebumps rose on my skin, my breath slipping out in dense clouds of fog.

"What's happening?" one of the Lolita girls asked.

A bright blue light began to emanate from the room. Along with it, a strange wind began to blow.

Master Qiang chanted louder.

"Jesus, what in the hell is that?" one of the werewolves asked.

The air grew even colder, and ice began to form on the pipes overhead. I looked back at Agent Keung.

"*Elemental,*" he mouthed.

The light grew brighter. Master Qiang spoke loudly, his voice firm and demanding. Light flashed, and for a brief moment, the debris on the ground lifted a few feet in the air then slowly settled back down.

Then, I heard a soft, hissing voice.

"Alodie," one of the Lolitas whispered, fear in her voice.

Master Qiang spoke in Chinese once more, his tone loud and commanding.

The strange voice hissed in reply. Then there was a whooshing sound and a blast of white light. Everything grew dark.

"Alodie, what's happening?" one of the werewolves whispered.

The little girl cried softly.

"Master Qiang?" Alodie demanded.

"He is looking. Be silent."

The werewolves stilled. There was no sound save the soft sobs of Master Qiang's granddaughter.

A moment later, the blue light returned, bringing the cold and wind along with it.

The voice spoke in a hiss once more.

"Well, did it find him? What is he saying?" Alodie asked.

Master Qiang did not answer.

"Master Qiang," Alodie demanded.

"Look," Master Qiang retorted sharply.

"Alodie, the map," one of the Lolitas said.

Alodie gasped excitedly. "There. There you are. Well done, Master Qiang. We got what we wanted. Dismiss your monster."

"And if I do not?"

There was a soft cry from the unseen child. "Then I guess we'll see which of us is faster."

I looked at Keung. "Now or never," I said in a whisper.

He nodded.

I pulled the hammers back on my pistols.

"What was that?" one of the Lolitas asked.

Agent Keung and I stepped into the room.

"Agent Louv—" the Lolita began, but her voice died in her throat as I shot.

I turned my guns on the guard who was shifting form. The other Lolita moved to intercept Keung who readied his blade.

"No. Keung, stop," Master Qiang called.

I looked from the shaman to the torrent of blue light. Inside was a monster. A creature with long, flowing hair, horns, and silver eyes glared out. Blue, white, and silver light twisted around the creature.

"Kill the wolves," Master Qiang commanded the creature.

Alodie, her eyes glimmering red, glanced around the

room. Her eyes stopped on a map resting on a dilapidated table at the center of the room. I followed her gaze. The map showed a line that began in the American southwest and snaked across the country, the ocean, toward Europe. There was a strange symbol thereon. In the vast wasteland of the American west, lit by the same unholy bluish light that surrounded Master Qiang's spirit creature, was a wolf head wearing a crown.

"Louvel, you menace," Alodie said with a sneer. She'd been holding the shaman's granddaughter in front of her. When the monster turned toward her, she shoved the girl to the floor.

Quickly shifting form into a wolf—a large beast with pure white hair—she dodged around both me and the monster, jumping onto the table and snatching the map in her maw. She raced from the room. The monster Master Qiang controlled blasted around the room in a torrent of light and cold. The monster grabbed the werewolf before me and devoured it. The werewolf was sucked into the vortex of light and simply disappeared. The creature then turned toward the Lolita.

Shaking myself from the sight, I turned and raced after Alodie.

Just as I reached the exit, the pipe on the ceiling over me finally cracked. A cascade of ice-cold water showered all over me, drenching me in near-freezing water. I gasped. Shaken for a moment, I rushed out onto the street. I arrived just in time to see the auto turn the corner at the end of the block. Alodie was gone.

CHAPTER 3
Wherefore Art Thou, Lionheart?

P romising to give me an update on what he learned from the shaman, Agent Keung headed back across town with Master Qiang and his granddaughter. The little girl had enough for one night. I didn't want to delay in getting her home and safe. With the pair safely bestowed with Agent Keung, I headed in the direction of Temple Square. Things were getting out of hand. I could only guess who Alodie was hunting. Maybe Lionheart knew something I didn't. And even if he didn't know, he needed to leave whatever library he was hunkered down in and get to work keeping things in order.

I worked my way down the Strand to the entrance of Temple Square. By the time I reached the square, I was mostly dry once again. Dry, but cold. Part of me entertained the idea that maybe Lionheart would invite me in for a hot toddy. But I also reminded myself that I was now spoken for. I had no business going anywhere with Lionheart unless it was to arrest someone.

Two Templar wolves were standing guard at the gate, which was kept closed these days. The heightened security on the square had become a common fixture these last few months. The wolves moved to meet me.

"Good evening, Agent Louvel," one of them said.

"I'm here to see Lionheart."

"The alpha doesn't wish to be disturbed right now," the wolf replied stiffly.

"I'm sure he doesn't. Neither do I, but I'm disturbed all the same. Realm issues, of course. I hate to be a nuisance, but it is rather important. Perhaps someone can check if he has a moment for me."

The wolf looked to his companion who nodded. Without another word, the Templar pack member turned and headed back into the square. My eyes trailed him as he went. To my surprise, he headed into the cathedral.

I turned to the guard. "I don't think we've met. You are Sir…"

"Nash."

"Sir Nash," I said with a nod. "I'm Clemeny."

"I know who you are, Agent Louvel," he said stiffly.

While Lionheart and I had always gotten along, the other pack members had clearly not warmed up to me.

But then again, maybe *I* wasn't the problem. The Templars had never had an alpha, had never led the packs. In fact, for the most part, they functioned independently of the werewolves in the realm, minding their own tasks. The mess with Cyril had all but halted their daily lives, a routine they had followed for decades. But they could hardly blame me. It was Victoria who'd done the asking; I was just the messenger.

I heard the cathedral door open. A moment later, two figures crossed the square toward me once more. The guard was returning and with him…wasn't Lionheart.

Instead, the beta of the Templar pack, Sir Blackwood, approached.

He motioned to the other wolves who left.

"Agent Louvel," he said, inclining his head to me. Sir Harlan Blackwood was tall, dark-haired, and essentially humorless. I had dealt with him on just a few occasions. He was a man—well, werewolf—of few words. Unlike many of the other Templars who found work at King's College, Sir Blackwood still had some dealings with Rome about which I knew almost nothing. But Lionheart trusted him. So, despite my own misgivings, so did I—kind of.

"Good evening, Sir Blackwood. I was hoping to speak to Lionheart."

He nodded. Once. "He's not available."

"Very well. Can you relay a message?"

Again, one nod.

"Talkative, aren't you, Sir Blackwood?"

The comment, at least, earned me a slight smile. Not a bad sight on his square and rugged jaw.

"Lolitas are involved in something. Some of Cyril and Fenton's old dogs are back and working with her. She lifted a shaman from Limewood, used him to help her track someone in the Americas. I do believe she's up to no good."

"Then it's a good thing we have the Red Capes to protect the realm. I will relay your message. Goodnight, Agent Louvel."

"Sir Blackwood," I said with a nod.

I cast a glance behind me as I left, reaching out with my sixth sense, feeling for Lionheart. The palms of my hand prickled. He was there. Why hadn't he come?

"Sir Blackwood," I called to the knight, who was headed back toward the chapel.

He stopped and looked back at me, his eyes flashing red in the darkness.

"Yes?"

"Is Sir Richard well?"

Again—infuriatingly—he nodded. Once.

Frustration boiled up in me, but I kept a lid on it.

"Please send him my regards," I said then turned and left.

All right, Lionheart. What's going on? He was there, but he was…ignoring me? Indisposed? Sick? I didn't know what, but an unsettled alpha is an unsettled realm, the last thing I needed when a bitch was about to stir up some trouble.

CHAPTER 4

A Rose is a Rose is a Rose

It was nearly five in the morning when I left Temple Square. It was far too early to stop by Grand-mère's flat. Of course, she wouldn't complain about me waking her—much—but I couldn't help but notice that she was slower to rise each morning as the years progressed. No, I still had work to do. Since Lionheart was going to be of no help whatsoever, I headed instead to headquarters.

First, I needed to pull up our records on the American werewolf population. I knew a little about the key players, but the American werewolves rarely jumped the pond. As it was, they were too busy terrorizing New York City to be bothered with London. Then again, Alodie wasn't interested in New York. That map had shown a symbol somewhere in the west, New Mexico or

Arizona. At least, that's where the strange blue line had started. It had moved across the page, crossing the Atlantic. I frowned. What in the hell was Alodie tracking? I would begin making inquiries with my counterparts in the United States at the Federal Bureau of Supernatural Affairs. Maybe they knew something. And second, I needed to track Alodie. While Victoria had let the Lolitas stay after the purge, Lionheart had closed Alodie's brothel. She'd gone to ground since. Now she had some plans in the works. I needed to find out what those plans were.

I took a tram back to headquarters, the car lurching to a stop when I arrived, my stomach shaking along with it. Taking the lift, I headed upstairs. It was so quiet that I could hear the ticking of the clock on the wall. The globes on the lamps hanging from above cast a warm, orange glow around the room. Only one other desk lamp was lit, but otherwise the workroom was empty.

I headed to the records room. During regular working hours, someone would be here to assist me with finding files. But this was the graveyard shift. The room was lined from floor to ceiling with drawers. Luckily, I knew my own department's records like my own name. As I pulled open a drawer, which seemed to extend at least three feet into the wall, I sent a silent blessing to Quinn and his old partner, Agent Jamison, for keeping everything in order. My fingers danced across the files until I reached the section on the American werewolf packs.

Snapping open the file, I pulled off my eyepatch and slipped it into my pocket. I was wearing it less and less these days. I was getting used to my new face, and in truth, I could see much better without the eyepatch. My mooneye had its own way of seeing, which wasn't without benefits.

I flipped through the papers, searching for any connection. There was nothing current. Some wolves had left Britain and gone to the colonies early on. They'd tangled with the native preternaturals but had eventually blended in. There were no links back to the London packs that I could find. But still, something nagged on my mind. There was a connection there, but I couldn't quite remember.

"At work already?" a masculine voice asked from behind me.

I closed my eyes and inhaled deeply. Cinnamon.

"Can't slouch on the job. Might upset my boss," I said.

Edwin took me by the waist and gently turned me toward him. I glanced up at him, the butterflies in my stomach doing an embarrassing amount of acrobatics. Edwin reached up and stroked my cheek, his finger gently caressing the scar below my eye.

"And just what are you searching for at this ungodly hour?" he asked.

"Bad people doing bad things."

"Indeed?"

Shut up and kiss me. Shut up and kiss me. "Wild West style, I think."

"That's new."

"So it is. And what are you doing awake at this ungodly hour?"

He took his hand from my cheek to show me the tape thereon. "I was at the Society gymnasium beating inanimate objects."

"Feel better?"

"Much."

"And what brought you here?" I asked.

He grinned. "A hunch."

"Always with the hunches."

"They serve me well."

"Any hunches about anything else right now?" I asked, giving him a sly grin as I set my hand gently on his arm.

"Why, Agent Louvel, I do believe you're flirting with me."

"Then my skills must be improving. At least you can tell."

At that, he chuckled lightly then leaned in to set a

kiss on my lips, but no sooner had our lips touched, there was a loud clatter from somewhere down the hall. Edwin pulled back. He raised an eyebrow at me.

I set the file aside, pulled my gun, then followed the noise. Stepping quietly, Edwin and I made our way down the dark hall. As we did so, I spotted lamplight coming from the armory.

Metal clattered again, and this time, I heard a feminine voice cursing like a drunken sailor.

My pistol in front of me, I turned and stepped into the room.

Looking down the barrel of my pistol, I found myself face to face with a blood-spattered Agent Rose who was staring down the barrel of her own weapon at me.

"Clemeny," she said, heaving a sigh of relief. "I almost shot you."

"Same," I replied.

Agent Rose cast a glance at Agent Hunter. A flicker of surprise and then amusement crossed her face. "Sir, I didn't expect to find you here at this hour," she said, giving me a passing glance. She smirked.

"I had some work to do," Edwin replied. "Agent Rose, are you hurt?"

She looked down at her clothes. "No. That's not my blood. But I was about to go murder a whole nest of vampires. I'll be sure to complete my paperwork afterward," she told Agent Hunter with a wink. Then she turned to me. "Want to come? I could use an extra hand."

Like me, Agent Rose was still without a partner. I really didn't know much about her beat. Most of the agents who worked with vampires stayed out in the field. And Agent Rose had a tendency to do things the way she wanted, when she wanted, where she wanted, an attitude which had annoyed Agent Greystock—and now Agent Hunter. I was dead tired and had a ton of work to do, but my curiosity was piqued.

"I take it my silver bullets won't work," I said.

"They will sting a bit but not kill. But these will," she said, bending to pick a metal box up off the ground. She opened it and handed two daggers to me, both had metal handles, the blades made out of wood.

I glanced at Edwin who was unable to hide the worry that crossed his features.

"Agent Hunter, while I'm out, would you please assign some junior agents to do surveillance at the airship towers. I need eyes on the lookout for Alodie," I said.

"Alodie?" he asked, raising an eyebrow.

"Unfortunately. I believe that bitch is about to blow up the realm, so to speak. I need to make sure she doesn't leave the country. If anyone spots her, have them arrest her and bring her in for questioning."

"Of course."

"Thank you," I told him, reaching out to brush his hand with the tips of my fingers.

He inclined his head to me. I could see in his eyes that he wanted to say something, do something, but our relationship was still a secret. Edwin wasn't sure how the others would take the news that we were attached. It would come out into the open sooner or later, and we would deal with it then. Then, but not yet.

I turned back to Agent Rose. "Lead the way."

Agent Rose pulled another two daggers from the box, shoved them into her belt, then grabbed a vial which she stuffed into her satchel.

"Sir," she said, inclining her head to Agent Hunter. She made her way out of the room.

I smiled softly at Edwin.

He pointed at the daggers in my hand. "Right in the heart. And…be careful."

Nodding to him, I slipped Agent Rose's daggers into my belt and headed out behind her. I was about to go fight a monster with which I had no experience while working with an agent who was known for being a smidgen reckless. What could go wrong?

I cast a glance back over my shoulder toward the armory. Edwin stood in doorway watching us go. Well, at the very least, someone cared if I lived or died. A warm feeling filled my chest, and I suppressed the schoolgirlish sigh that wanted to escape my lips. *No time for that, Clemeny.* Because if *my* hunch was right, things were about to get messy.

CHAPTER 5
A Rose by Any Other Name

Agent Rose and I took the lift to the upper floor of headquarters which looked to the untrained eye like any random townhouse on any random street in one of the sleepiest districts of London. The lift from our underground headquarters to the townhouse was disguised as a broom cupboard. Slipping between the pails and mops, Agent Rose and I exited the closet into a foyer between the kitchen and the parlor of the townhouse.

The sound of the closet door opening summoned a maid, who was actually a trained agent, from the kitchen.

"Ah, Agents Rose and Louvel. Breakfast before you head out, Agents?" Annabeth, the house agent, asked. "I have tea on."

"No, thank you," Agent Rose answered for both of us.

My stomach, which growled hungrily at the mere thought of food, was inclined to disagree, but Agent Rose seemed like she was in a hurry.

"Very well. Perhaps a handkerchief, Agent Rose?" Annabeth said, offering a pretty, lace-trimmed handkerchief to Agent Rose.

She smirked then took the dainty handkerchief.

I tapped on my cheek to indicate where she had the splatter. As she wiped it off, I eyed her over. Agent Rose was, in fact, very attractive. With pale blonde hair, blue eyes, and very red lips, her looks were more fitting for the social set. But there was a stony hardness behind her gaze which I knew well. Something was motivating her. There was a reason she was at the agency and not sitting around playing the pianoforte all day. I knew that sharp edge because it was a mirror of my own. The flavor was, perhaps, a bit different. But it was there all the same.

She wiped the blood off—the droplets leaving a faint echo of stain on her pale cheeks—then handed the cloth back to the maid.

"Thanks," she said then turned and headed to the front door.

Pausing a minute, I turned to the maid. "Scones?" I whispered.

She nodded. "Blueberry."

Dammit. I cringed.

"I'll save you one, Agent Louvel."

"Thanks," I said then turned and went after Agent Rose who was waiting for me at the door.

"Best not to eat until after," Agent Rose told me.

We headed outside where Agent Rose had a steamauto waiting.

"Agents," Thomas, the other another residential agent playing servant, said as we emerged. Dressed like an ordinary servant, save the pistols at his side and in his boot, he was lighting the lamp outside the townhouse.

"Good morning, Thomas," I said.

"Louvel and Rose together. God help them," he said with a chuckle.

"It's not God they need to worry about," Agent Rose said with a laugh as we headed toward the auto.

I slipped into the passenger seat, strapping myself in and keeping my opinion about the infernal machine to myself. Rose adjusted a few levers, the engine boiling and hissing, then set off across town.

"So, who are we smiting?" I asked.

"A month back, Lady Caroline Graham made a visit to Bath, her niece Penelope along with her. Penelope was enamored by some traveling entertainers that passed through. She frequented the show. Unfortunately, when the cirque left, so did Penelope."

"And I take it our entertainers have rather extraordinary talents."

"They do, and they're a damned menace. I tracked them back to London. They've rented an old theater. I was waiting for the sun before I went to have a look. We need to see if Penelope is still amongst the living. And if not, kindly murder her. Otherwise, we'll ship the performers back to Europe where they came from or smite them, whichever comes first.

"Sounds like a plan."

We headed across town to an area well known for live entertainment, from opera to burlesque. The group Agent Rose described would certainly blend in well here, except for the fact that they're all undead. She pulled her auto to a stop not far from the old theater. The boiler hissed.

Agent Rose eyed the sky. Soft shades of orange and pink lit up the horizon.

"How many?" I asked.

"Seven, unless Penelope is turned, which would make eight. At least four are very old."

"I take it the older, the stronger?"

She nodded.

"Just like wolves."

Agent Rose slipped out of the auto and went to the

back. I followed her. She opened the boot to reveal an arsenal. Guns, bombs, knives, and every other imaginable device of destruction were stashed inside.

"Hell's bells," I whispered. "I think we just became best friends."

Agent Rose grinned. "Lots to choose from, but I was out of consecrated stakes," she said, tapping her belt.

"These are nice," I said, touching a set of knuckle-busters.

"Take them. They're silver-plated," she said, untying the knuckles and handing them to me.

I slipped them on. "I do believe we're engaged, Agent Rose."

She laughed. "Sorry, Louvel. I'm already married. Let's go," she said, closing the boot with a click.

"Wait, what?"

Agent Rose smirked but didn't answer me.

We headed toward the theater. Of course, the front door is never the way to go. I eyed the entrances. There was an entrance underground at the side of the building, but underground and vampires seemed like a terrible idea. A ladder led to the roof above.

"There," I said, pointing.

Agent Rose nodded, and we headed to the side of the building. Jumping, Agent Rose caught the bottom rung of the ladder and pulled herself up. I followed along behind her.

As we climbed up, my scalp got a strange, tingly feeling and my palms began to itch. Oh yeah, something was definitely off here.

We slipped onto the roof then looked around. A door led to the attic. Agent Rose motioned to me, and we headed to it. Slipping my blade into the doorframe, I popped the lock, and Agent Rose and I headed inside.

When Agent Rose pulled her wooden stake dagger, I did the same.

I was suddenly missing my furry friends.

"How's Quinn?" Agent Rose asked. Soft morning light shone in through the dusty attic windows. The wood on the walls, floors, and even ceiling were a pale ash color. Trunks were stacked in one corner, a row of costumes covered in inches of dust on the other side. Stage props made of decaying paper-mâché stunk of must and looked like the rats had been working on them.

"Better. Recovering still. I'll be seeing him soon," I whispered, wondering if it really was the best time for conversation. Didn't fangs have enhanced hearing like wolves? Maybe it didn't matter if they were sleeping. But mention of my plans to go to Twickenham filled my stomach with nervous excitement. I had invited Edwin to come with me. Quinn had met Edwin only briefly when Edwin was in charge of Shadow Watch. This time,

I'd be introducing my former partner and friend to my beau.

"Tell him I send my greetings. I thought they landed you with Harper."

"She's on rotation. Wouldn't mind having her back though."

Agent Rose huffed a little laugh. "Good to have someone watching your back, I guess," she said but didn't add anything else. My brow furrowed as I considered her words. Her manner suggested she preferred working the job alone, but I also knew that she and Agent Reid had been close. Agent Rose was a puzzle.

We reached the door on the other side of the attic and headed downstairs.

There was a soft breeze as the air in the theater blew up the steps. I listened for the sound of anything, but it was deadly silent. We exited the steps to find ourselves in the backstage area. Working quietly, we headed down a hall until we found ourselves front and center on the old stage.

The stage looked out at rows of seats upholstered in red velvet. There was a balcony at the back of the theater. There were large, arched windows along the walls. Heavy drapes covered them, shutting out the light. Only one window, where the fabric had ripped at the top, allowed in some sunshine. Motes of dust danced through the air as a single beam of light shown down on the theater aisle.

But the most interesting fixture in the room was the eight coffins that lined the stage.

Hell's bells.

Grinning, Agent Rose turned and look back at me. She pulled a wooden dagger from her belt and gave it a flip. "Ready for some fun?"

Agent Rose approached the coffins slowly. "Look at the designs," she whispered. "These are the oldest," she said, pointing to the wooden boxes. I could see what she meant. While the wood on some of the coffins looked relatively new, the older coffins had older, expensive looking wood that was more elaborately carved.

"Okay, Penelope, where are you? Eeny, meeny, miny, moe," Agent Rose whispered, her finger bouncing as she stood behind two newer looking coffins. Ending the rhyme, she motioned to a coffin made of fresh-cut lumber.

Holding her wooden dagger, she motioned to me.

I readied myself, holding the stake in front of me.

Moving quickly, Agent Rose slid the lid off the coffin.

There was a strange, screeching scream, and a moment later, a young woman leaped from the coffin and lunged at Agent Rose. The movement was so quick, it caught me off guard. The girl's black hair was a long, tangled mess. Her face was white as milk, her nails long and sharp.

I moved to help Agent Rose but heard the sound of wood scraping behind me.

"Clemeny, look out," Agent Rose called as she flung the vampiress who had attacked her to the ground. Agent Rose jumped on the vampire, pinning her to the ground.

I looked behind me to find a male vampire slipping out of his coffin. He was tall, lean, and had beautiful golden hair and the brightest blue eyes I had ever seen. He tipped his head sideways as he looked at me.

He breathed in deeply then stared at me, his brow scrunching up like he was perplexed. "Like red roses," he whispered. "Who are you?"

Behind me, the vampiress Agent Rose was wrestling screeched.

The male vampire looked around me at Agent Rose.

Not missing my chance, I gripped the wooden dagger and attacked, slamming the stake into the vampire's chest.

The vampire looked from the stake in his chest to me.

"They call me Little Red," I said with a grin.

The vampire's eyes met mine, and a moment later, he exploded.

Literally, exploded.

Hell's bells.

Blood, body parts, and unnamed everything splattered everywhere. In disbelief, I stood staring at the heap of blood and guts on the ground—and all over me.

Behind me, I heard a scream then a similar wet, popping sound.

Agent Rose sighed then joined me, looking down at the mess at my feet.

"That's why I said to wait for breakfast," Agent Rose said with a smirk as she wiped off her hands. I looked over my shoulder to see a pulpy mess on the floor where the female vampire had been.

"Not Penelope," she said, motioning to what was left of the corpse of the female vampire. She paused a moment then picked a lump of something from my hair. "Sorry, should have warned you. They called that one Vincent," she said, flicking the piece of Vincent to the ground. "He must have been a light sleeper," she said then handed a pouch to me. "These will make it easier."

I looked down at my clothes. "He got Fenton dirty," I said, wiping a hunk of Vincent off the tuft of Fenton's hide I wore on my belt.

At that, Agent Rose laughed.

Shaking off the gore, I opened the bag Agent Rose had given me. Inside were nails. "Nails?"

"Consecrated. One per coffin will work. Might wake them up though. You'll want to be ready," she said then headed over to the biggest and oldest coffin. Climbing on top, she set one of the nails on the coffin lid, and taking the butt of her gun, hammered it in.

I started work on another. I had just hammered the coffin lid closed when the coffin beside me began to open.

"Agent Rose," I called.

Rose jumped from the coffin she was working on.

A moment later, the lid slid off the coffin and moving quickly, a man leaped from the coffin. His pale eyes flashed as he looked from me to Agent Rose.

"Briar Rose," he hissed.

Reaching inside her vest, Agent Rose grabbed something and threw it across the ground between us and the vampire. At first, I wasn't sure what it was. All three of us stood looking at the shimmering substance lying there. A moment later, I realized it was sand.

"Now, that's just dirty," the vampire hissed. Bending down, I watched in fascination as the vampire began to slowly count the grains of sand.

"Where's Penelope?" Agent Rose asked.

"Why would I tell you?"

Agent Rose reached into her pocket and sprinkled a little more sand onto the ground.

The vampire sighed loudly. "Rude."

"Mind buttoning up the rest?" she asked, pointing to the remaining coffins.

I nodded.

"Who is she?" the vampire asked, looking at me.

"None of your business."

Hammering in the next nail, my senses were alive as I listened for any sound of anything. The last thing I wanted was another exploding vampire. I looked down at my clothes. They were going to need a soak.

"And Penelope?" Agent Rose asked again.

"Dirty Red Cape. We know who you are."

"And yet you still crossed paths with me," Agent Rose retorted.

I grinned.

Moving to put a nail in the next coffin, I discovered that the pine box was already nailed shut.

"Problem," I said.

Agent Rose looked at me.

"Already closed."

"Ah, that would be Penelope," she said then turned and joined me. "Keep an eye on him. The sand should keep him entertained for the next several days but still."

Pulling an iron from her bag, Agent Rose slowly worked on the coffin, removing the lid.

I eyed the vampire warily. There was cold hatred in his eyes as he stared at Agent Rose.

The lid of the coffin flew off with a clatter.

"Here we go. Penelope, my dear, you look dreadful," Agent Rose said then leaned over the unseen body. After a moment, she leaned back up. "Dammit."

"Too late?" I asked.

Agent Rose shook her head. "Infected, but not turned yet."

"She's a present," the vampire said with a malicious smile.

"For whom?" Agent Rose asked.

He laughed. "Take a guess."

Agent Rose frowned at him.

"Can she be saved?" I asked.

"Yes, but it will be long and painful," Agent Rose said then turned back to the vampire counting the grains of sand. "I asked for who?" she said, kicking the fang over.

"Someone you know very well," he said with a hissing laugh.

"Shite," Agent Rose swore, her face screwing up with frustration. She pulled her dagger from her belt and without a second thought, she stabbed the vampire in the heart.

Turning in time, I shielded myself from the splatter.

Agent Rose sighed heavily then went to the last

coffins and finished off sealing them with the consecrated nails.

I stared from the mess that had been the vampire to the open coffin. Moving carefully, I walked over and looked into the coffin wherein I saw one of the prettiest girls I'd ever seen in my life. Lying on a bed of silk and dressed in blue, her curly black hair framing her face, she looked like a porcelain doll.

Her breathing was shallow.

I stared at her. On her neck, I saw the distinct mark of a vampire bite.

Startling me, the girl took a raspy, shuttering breath. Her blue eyes opened wide. At first, they were the same icy blue as the vampire, Vincent, but they darkened to a stormy blue-green with flecks of brown.

"S-save me," the girl whispered.

On hearing her, Agent Rose rushed across the room. Working carefully, she helped the girl out of the coffin.

"It's all right, Miss Graham. We're here to help. We'll take you somewhere safe," Agent Rose reassured her as she aided the girl to her feet. I was surprised to hear softness in Agent Rose's voice.

"I was in Bath," the girl said, her voice trembling. She slipped on some vampire gore as she stepped out. The girl looked back, a confused look on her face as she studied the blood on the ground. Her eyes went to the coffin. "Is that… Is that a casket?"

"No, no," I lied. "Don't be ridiculous."

"Clemeny, can you take her to my auto?"

I eyed the bite mark on the girl's neck. "Is she dangerous?"

Agent Rose shook her head. "No. She wasn't turned, just infected."

"You sure?"

Agent Rose smirked then looked away from me. "Very sure. Take her outside. I'll settle things in here," Agent Rose said.

I nodded. Helping the girl down the steps and off the stage, I led her through the theater.

Behind us, Agent Rose went to the windows and began tearing off the drapes. The old fabric ripped loudly, the material falling down in a dusty flutter. Sunlight shined into the theater.

"My eyes hurt," Penelope whispered, wincing.

I reached into my bag, fishing around for my old goggles lying at the bottom. I hadn't used them since before the accident. I kept meaning to take them out but never bothered. "Here," I said, handing them to her.

She frowned at them a little then put them on.

I chuckled to myself. We'd just saved her from a nest of vampires, and she was turning her nose up at the fashion of my goggles? Figures.

I led the girl outside then helped Penelope into the

auto. Agent Rose exited the theater a few minutes later. She paused to barricade the doors.

"Settled?" I asked.

She nodded. "I'll send around a crew to mop up the mess then ship what's left of this lot back home."

I cast a glance at Penelope. "And her?"

Agent Rose sighed. "I'll see to her."

"Then I'll find my way home from here."

Agent Rose nodded. "Thanks for your help."

"Of course."

"Be careful, Clemeny."

"You too…Briar?"

She smirked then slipped into the driver's seat. "I'm only a Briar to them," she said then started the engine which hissed, a puff of steam streaming out into the morning air. "It's Aurora." Waving with a single finger, she turned and drove off.

I looked down at my clothes. I was suddenly very glad that I hadn't eaten the blueberry scone after all. If I had, I'd be covered in scone and Vincent.

Sighing, I cast a glance around to get my bearings then headed home, hoping to catch a ride back across the river.

CHAPTER 6
What Missus Coleridge Doesn't Know

Slipping in through the window of my flat at Missus Coleridge's, I tiptoed across the floor, so the boards wouldn't squeak. Thus far, Missus Coleridge hadn't gotten wise to my new trick. I strongly suspected that if she knew I was scaling the nearby building, then using a plank to cross between the two structures and climbing into my window just to avoid questions, she might just turn me out. Part of me dreamed of the moment when I landed on Edwin's doorstep with nowhere else to go. It would be a shame to have to spend a luxurious hour soaking in the claw-footed bathtub I imagined he owned. The bath would be followed, of course, by the rest of the morning spent under the sheets with that excellent man. But, alas. Thus far, I hadn't gotten more than a kiss out of my new beau. And as for that bathtub…

I scanned my small flat. In the corner, water dripped from the ceiling into a bucket. I'd stopped asking where the water was coming from. It hardly mattered anymore. I was just here to wash off the muck and get some sleep. As soon as I got a little rest, I'd be back to tracking down Alodie.

I looked at my clothes. I really was a mess. No wonder I couldn't even get the coal wagon to give me a ride.

I stripped off everything, surprised to find the gore had seeped down to my bodice and nickers. I'd always wondered about Agent Rose's beat. Curiosity sated. She could keep her exploding fangs. I filled a bucket with soapy water and washed out my clothes, hanging them on a line stretched across the length of my small flat to dry. Quickly wiping off the armor, I reminded myself to polish the metal when I woke up. I gave my blade a sloppy clean then set it aside. I'd need to work on it later. I was so tired my eyes were closing. Pulling out a sponge, I washed my hair and gave myself a good scrub, rubbing my tired limbs with some gardenia lotion Grand-mère had given me three Christmases back. I couldn't remember if I'd ever used it before. I grabbed the chemise I'd dug out of my wardrobe when I had considered, albeit briefly, wearing a dress to Quinn's. Even though I'd already given up the idea, I hadn't had time to pack the elegant ladies' clothes back into the cupboard.

I lay down on my thin bed and closed my eyes. Thoughts of Edwin drifted through my mind. Suddenly, I envisioned him and me in that tub together, the warm water lapping around me, and Edwin's arms embracing me.

RM

I WOKE I DON'T KNOW HOW MANY HOURS LATER TO THE sound of a brush scrubbing metal. My head was hazy. At first, I thought the odd sound was coming from the hallway. It only took a moment to realize the noise was coming from *inside* my room. I moved to grab my pistol, which had been sitting beside my bed, only to find it was gone. I sat up with a start, ready to kill whatever had found me, only to find Lionheart sitting there.

He was working a brush across my vambrace, gingerly holding the silver armor with a gloved hand. He paused to rub the metal with oil. My dagger, pistols, and other weapons had already been cleaned and polished. He looked up at me from under a lock of blond hair.

"You should clean your gear before you sleep," he said.

"I was tired."

He lifted the vambrace, brushing off something red and sticky. "Anyone I know?"

I shook my head. "A fang."

Lionheart grinned his wolfy half-smile that always evoked an inappropriate rush of energy through my body.

As if reading my thoughts, his eyes drifted toward me.

It slowly dawned on me that I was half-naked. I glanced down at my loose chemise. The pale apricot fabric did very little to hide what was underneath. My chest half hanging out, my breasts pressing against the sheer fabric, Lionheart had just gotten more of an eyeful than any man alive.

Smiling lightly, he averted his eyes then turned back to his work.

My heart thundered in my chest, and a hundred inappropriate thoughts raced through my mind. It took every ounce of me to remind myself that I was attached to Edwin Hunter and that I liked Bryony Paxton.

Lionheart rose and sat down at the foot of my bed. He handed the vambrace to me then studied my face as he pulled off the gloves.

As I met his eyes, I realized that there was a ring of grey around his blue irises, a small scar by his eyebrow. If one didn't know better, if one didn't realize, he would seem entirely human. In truth, he had been. He was just different now.

Lionheart reached out and gently stroked my long hair, pushing it behind my shoulder which he touched lightly.

My heart beat hard.

"That's a very nice dress," he said, looking briefly over his shoulder at the gown hanging there. "Going somewhere?"

"Just an outing."

"With?"

"With someone. You're distracting me."

"From what?"

"From the fact that I'm angry with you."

"Are you? I always thought you looked like you could use a little distraction, Agent Louvel."

"Perhaps, but I like to choose what I'm distracted by."

"And?"

"And I maintain that letting you distract me is a terrible idea."

"But *you* are very distracting. And this mix of gardenia oil and your lovely rosy scent is more distracting than I care to admit."

I swallowed hard, ignoring the image of me pulling Lionheart down on top of me, the thoughts of my tongue roving around his mouth, and the feel of him between my legs.

Hell's bells, Clemeny. Get yourself together.

"Then, perhaps, you shouldn't come crawling through my window."

"I didn't. I came in through the front door."

"Good lord, I hope Missus Coleridge didn't see you."

Lionheart huffed a laugh. "I sneaked past a Saracen camp once. I think I can get around Missus Coleridge."

I gave him a wry grin. "Good. Now, before something regrettable happens, tell me why you're here."

"I owe you an explanation."

"Yes, you do."

Lionheart sighed. "My pack is unhappy."

"Why?"

"Because they don't want to marshal the realm. They want to continue to do their work uninterrupted by nonsense."

"Nonsense like the return of Fenton and Cyril's old dogs?"

"Yes."

"And Alodie up to…something?"

"Indeed."

"They do know they are still under a mandate from the Queen."

"They do, but they are not happy about it. And honestly, neither am I. I am also...distracted."

There was that word again. "By?"

"Bryony..."

Ah. My stomach twisted into a hard, jealous knot. To my surprise, my brow flexed with annoyance. I did like her. I did. It's just...

"With Alodie plotting, I'm concerned. I don't want anything to happen to her. Bryony is an innocent in all this...mess," Lionheart said.

His words hung heavy in the air between us. It was no business of mine that his heart was set on her. And Lionheart's distance had allowed me to set aside my unspoken, unwanted, and confusing feelings for him. In that space, Edwin had filled my heart. And I liked Bryony. I did. I do. I just... But this time, I realized a truth. Sir Richard Spencer also felt this strange struggle when it came to me. That was why this big, bad wolf was such a terrible temptation. That was also why he was here, at least in part.

"I see," I said, forcing out the words.

"I... I had a family once, very long ago. My wife and son perished while I was with King Richard. They died in a fire. I wasn't there. I did nothing to protect them. They too were innocents. They died while I was away doing the bidding of my monarch. And then God saw fit to turn me into this," he said, a tinge of angry disgust in his voice. "I can't let something happen to Bryony because of me. Do you understand?"

"I do, but stepping down or pulling back won't help. If anything, now is the time to show this realm you are the alpha. Alodie is a sneak, and she is plotting something. We need to stop her before she gets whatever plan she has underway. You must show them all once and for all that if they trifle with you, there will be a reckoning."

"Or, I need to cut a deal."

"Do you think Cyril's old dogs will let you back away? You know better, Richard. And that's beneath you. They will come for you all the same."

"Not if I'm gone. Not if I leave things to Sir Blackwood."

"Then they will come for your brothers instead. I know you won't allow that either. The Templars must show they rein control. If you don't, there will be chaos. You aren't thinking clearly."

Lionheart looked up at me again from under that lock of hair. There was a vulnerability in his expression which I had never seen before. His eyes danced across me. "Clearly not."

I smirked. "Stop that. You already have enough relational troubles. Maybe being a knight cost you in the past—and I am truly sorry for it—but now you need to be the knight you are. This is no time to retreat. I know your brothers would rather be buried in books, but the Dís said it well. Until you show your teeth, they will test you."

"The Dís? You spoke with the Dís?"

I nodded.

"I didn't know she was awake this year."

"That she is."

"And she speaks to you?"

I shrugged.

Lionheart huffed. "Interesting. Have you gone to the summer country, as I advised you?"

"I'm too busy cleaning up your messes."

Lionheart grinned then rose. He went to the window and looked out. "Nice view of the factory. Why do you live here, of all places?"

"You're changing the subject."

"Perhaps. But this place? Why?"

"The river throws off my scent. I don't want anyone finding their way to my grand-mère ever again."

"You'd be safer on holy ground."

"Well, if I see a chapel come up on the market, I'll be sure to buy it. Enough avoiding the point. What are you going to do?"

"I'll do as you suggest, on one condition," he said then turned. He crossed the room and stood in front of the gown hanging on the door to my wardrobe. It was a pretty dress, pale blue with lace at the bodice.

"Yes?" I replied, eyeing him suspiciously.

"I want to see you in this. Though, I admit, red is a better color on you."

"Very funny. I was about to pack it away again."

Lionheart held the silk skirt in his hand, letting the fabric slide through his fingers. Once more, part of me that had no business thinking of him like that trembled.

"No, you should wear it," Lionheart said softly. "I'd very much like to see you in it."

I willed the butterflies in my stomach be still. "You'll rally the brothers and help me snuff out this mess?"

"Yes."

"All right. We have a deal."

At that, Lionheart smirked. "Good," he said then went to the door. He unlocked it then turned the handle so gently I didn't even hear a click. "Don't forget to lock it behind me. Never know what kind of monsters might be lurking about."

I grinned. "Goodbye, Sir Richard."

"Goodbye, Agent Louvel."

After Lionheart left, I slipped out of bed and went to the door, locking it once more. I listened for any sound of his footsteps on the stairs or in the hallway, but there was nothing. He really was bloody quiet. And complicated. And handsome. And very dangerous for me. I closed my eyes, a guilty feeling sweeping over me. Lionheart was a vexing, wolfy distraction. And one I didn't need. I had Edwin now. Lionheart was just...a problem. Right now, what we needed was to keep the realm in order. Right now, I need to stop Alodie. I also need to do my part in keeping Bryony safe—which included not getting into any indiscretions with her man. A twist of jealousy stabbed me.

I sighed.

Putting my feelings aside—but leaving the gown hanging outside the wardrobe all the same—I went to get redressed. I grinned as I glanced down at my perfectly polished gear. Time to get back to work.

CHAPTER 7
The Dark District

Navigating the dark district was not a task any Red Cape ever looked forward to. For one, just about every bad thing that lurked in the realm lived there. From indifferent to downright hostile, the preternaturals living there had little use for us. Those humans who traveled through these zones did so unknowingly, for the most part. The supernatural had always existed in our world, but they had worked hard to keep their true nature secret. If there was one thing that was universally true of mankind, humans did not like anyone who was an other. From vampire to werewolf to goblin, there were plenty of others living amongst us. Wisely, they had let the truth of their natures become the thing of fairy tales. Honestly, I didn't blame them for keeping their natures secret.

My senses on full alert, I entered the dark district.

BITCHES AND BRAWLERS

The alleyway was so narrow, the peaks of the medieval buildings leaning so close together, that you could barely tell it was daytime. My boots clicked softly on the cobblestone. The gas lamps here were still lit, but they were spaced far apart and cast weak shadows. I kept my head down and made my way into the dark district. Since her brothel closed, Alodie and her pack had retreated into the dark zone. Now I had to go figure out what she was doing.

I could feel eyes watching me from the darkened windows. A goblin wearing a heavy cloak sat in an alcove drinking. The heady scent of alcohol surrounding him burned my nose. He cast me a passing glance.

"Better take off that cloak, Agent," he said with a laugh. "Looks more like a bullseye."

I frowned at him and turned the corner. I didn't like his words, but he was right. Passing a rail thin woman who stopped and stared at me, her black eyes tracing my every step as she tittered madly. Dammit. Even if I found Alodie, everyone in the district would be whispering that I was there before I could get a look at what she was doing. I scanned the nearby buildings. There was a stack of crates sitting in the alley. At their peak, the buildings almost touched one another. Moving quickly, I climbed up the heap of boxes then scaled the side of the building, moving from one jutting stone to another, scaling the side of the building. Grabbing the roof peak, I pulled myself up onto the rooftop. My heart beat hard from the exertion. Clapping off my hands, I eyed the roofs of the dark district. Now I was on common ground. Turning, I headed across the rooftops to the building where Alodie was rumored to have taken up residence.

The hair on my scalp rose, the bottom of my feet and palms tingling, as I worked my way through the district. Scanning with my mooneye, I had to blink hard when my good eye spotted an empty street, yet my mooneye distinctly saw the shape of a woman moving down the lane. I could only make out her silhouette in the field of white, the shapes of the buildings looming around her. She wore a black dress and twirled a parasol. She was there and not there. I watched as the phantom turned the corner.

Wonderful. The last thing I needed was to tangle with a demon, specter, or some other unholy thing I knew nothing about how to handle. An elemental and an exploding vampire had been quite enough for this week already. And then there was the emotionally conflicted werewolf who was toying with my heart. The fact that Lionheart had once had a family whom he'd loved and lost moved me. But I needed to focus on the job, not on Lionheart's personal dilemmas. I had enough of my own.

With the phantom gone, I took a running jump and leaped across the alleyway, following the street to the spot where Alodie had been seen. The block where she'd taken up residence looked to be her regular speed. I noted a tavern, an opium den, and a brothel—but not *her* brothel.

I moved between the gables until I found a spot to hide with a good eye on the werewolf's new lair. Alodie's auto was parked outside a gaming house. Gambling was not much of an improvement over a brothel, but at least her work was now vertical. Pulling out my spyglass, I scanned the building. There were two werewolves guarding the door. They checked visitors entering the gaming house, including a group of drunk airship pirates. I eyed them over. Not Skollson's crew, thank god. Skollson had gone limping back to Oslo and hadn't been heard from since. So far, at least. No, these unfortunate souls appeared to be human.

The wolves were both heavily armed. One I recognized as part of Fenton's old pack. The other was a stranger. I panned my spyglass on the windows, looking past the curtains inside. People were playing cards at gaming tables, rolling dice, drinking, and smoking tobacco. No sign of Alodie or her girls. Her auto was there, so she was likely inside, but I didn't see her. I sighed. I really didn't want to be here after dark, but for now, I had to wait.

It was nearly dusk when I decided it was time to get the hell out of there. For all I knew, only Alodie's auto was there. There was no sign of the wolf. And as it was, my mooneye had spotted at least four more phantoms, some unidentifiable creature who sped faster than the common eye could detect, at least one vampire—and it was not my week for vampires—and what might have been a succubus. Alongside them, some of London's common criminals came and went like there was nothing abundantly wrong with this part of town. How could such clever operators be so blind?

I was just gathering up my things when the door to the gaming house opened. Alodie emerged with two of her girls and two more werewolves, both of which had served Fenton. Hell's bells, almost a dozen, if not more, of the old pack had returned.

"Tomorrow night," Alodie told Antoinette, her direct subordinate. "Seven o'clock sharp."

Antoinette nodded. "I'll see to it."

Alodie kissed the she-wolf on both cheeks, then Antoinette and the others slipped into the auto and drove off. Alodie turned and headed down the street back toward the city.

Slipping my spyglass onto my belt, I turned and went after her.

CHAPTER 8
Alodie

I followed Alodie who turned down alley after alley. She traveled the length of the dark district and back into the city again. It wasn't long before she approached a modest looking townhouse in an otherwise unremarkable neighborhood. The only thing that distinguished the place was the expensive auto sitting outside. Fluffing her hair, Alodie went to the door and knocked. After a few moments, a man appeared. He quickly ushered the she-wolf inside. It all happened so fast, I couldn't get a proper look at him. Maneuvering until I got a good spot for surveillance on the rooftop opposite the building Alodie had entered, I pulled out my spyglass and panned the windows.

I caught the faint sound of a paleophone, and could just make out the undertones of voices. A few moments later, a lamp sparked to life in an upper floor, causing the room to glow orange. Not long after, the man passed the window as he pulled off his shirt. I heard Alodie's soft laugh.

The lamp dimmed. While I couldn't see what was happening, not long after, I caught the faint sound of, um, acrobatics.

I frowned. That was fast. But what in God's name was Alodie doing with a human?

I scanned the street. It was surprisingly quiet.

Slipping back down to the street, I quietly opened the door of the auto and slipped inside. The machine was remarkably clean. I checked all the compartments, finding nothing telling. Reaching under the bench, however, I pulled out a case. Clicking it open, I flipped through the papers inside, all of which were addressed to a gentleman by the name of Phillip Phillips.

I chuckled softly. Mr. Phillips had some creative parents.

I scanned the documents. From what I could tell, a company by the name of The Yowie Corporation was seeking to buy out Phillip Phillips' Australian Trading Company, an airship merchant company based out of Sydney. I scanned through the documents, most of which were financial in nature. I also found travel documents in the case, as well as some letters to Mr. Phillips from The Yowie Corporation. One was dated almost a month back. In it, it outlined meetings between The

Yowie Corporation's London representative, Alodie Wolfe—*seriously, Alodie?*—and Mr. Phillips. The itinerary noted several dinners, a show at the Adelphi dated a week back, and other entertainments Miss Wolfe would provide Mr. Phillips.

Pulling out my journal, I noted down all the essential details, including Mr. Phillips' agenda for the rest of his stay in London. I then slipped the papers back in the case and under the seat once more. I climbed quietly out of the car and turned and headed back into the city.

So, a few things were becoming evident.

The Yowie Corporation was a front to get Fenton and Cyril's old dogs back into London. Buying a trading company gave them easy access back into the realm and money to boot. It hardly seemed like the kind of plan the old gang could concoct on their own. Alodie, however, was another matter. There was a reason she had survived Cyril's rein *and* managed to keep the peace with the Red Capes. She was smart and cunning, a terrible match.

But what was Alodie playing at? The realm had always been ruled by male alphas. Was Alodie planning a matriarchy? And how was all this tied to the American West? What, besides nocturnal acrobatics, was Alodie up to? And why was she playing that card anyway?

I pulled out my pocket watch and looked at the time.

It was nearly two in the morning. I was supposed to meet Edwin to make a mid-morning trip to Twickenham to visit Quinn and Jessica. Quinn, as much my protector as ever, had insisted that he get to know Edwin. While Grand-mère had given Edwin her approval almost immediately—a fact which raised my suspicions as to why Agent Greystock suggested Edwin for the job—Quinn would be far more cautious.

I looked over my notes. Phillip Phillips was scheduled to take a tour of the British Museum tomorrow afternoon. I needed to get a look at him, to determine if he was a werewolf, and try to get a sense of what Alodie was plotting. Maybe Edwin would be willing to join me for a tour of the museum. That was something real couples did, wasn't it? We'd be just another pair taking in the art. What was the harm in that? Now I just needed to convince Edwin to turn our romantic outing into an opportunity to hunt werewolves.

CHAPTER 9
The Infamous Missus Coleridge

I dragged myself back to Missus Coleridge's to get a little sleep before I needed to head back across town to meet Edwin. To my annoyance, I woke with thoughts of Lionheart dancing through my head. Problematic and utterly charming werewolf.

I rose and looked at the blue gown hanging there.

I had decided not to wear it. But now... If I was able to talk Edwin into a trip to the museum for a look around, I needed to play the part.

After I washed up, I redressed in the blue gown. I braided my long black hair and fixed it in a bun. Digging in the back of my wardrobe, I pulled out a hat box. Inside, I found the mini top hat Grand-mère had given me to go along with the gown. Made of matching blue fabric and adorned with peacock feathers, it was a pretty thing. The veil attached to the hat would even hide my mooneye. I pinned the hat on. I slipped my knife and Rose's knucklebusters into a hidden pocket in the gown, slid my pistols into my boots, and grabbed my satchel.

"Have to sit this one out, Fenton," I said, eyeing my gear, including Fenton's pelt, lying on my bed.

I went to my looking glass and took a glimpse.

I was surprised to see the old Clemeny, the pre-Red Cape Society Clemeny, staring back at me—well, all but the mangled face. In the years leading up to my joining the society, I was forever bored. I always felt like I was waiting for something amazing to happen, like I was destined to do more than marry Pastor Clark and his sardine breathe and go to high teas. I would be forever grateful to Eliza Greystock for recruiting me to the agency.

And now, it seemed, I had something else to be grateful to her for. After all, if she hadn't stepped down, I probably would never have met Edwin.

Grabbing my satchel—I couldn't bring myself to carry a reticule—I headed out the door, wincing as the stairs creaked when I reached the landing.

"Clemeny? Is that you?" Missus Coleridge called, her front door flying open.

I flinched. "Yes, Missus Coleridge."

"My girl, you're as quiet as a mouse. I never heard you come in last night. Well, well, well, look at you,"

Missus Coleridge said, her hands on her considerable hips as she eyed me over.

I smiled at Missus Coleridge who was wearing so much face paint and lipstick that she reminded me of a vaudevillian. She was dressed in her favorite brown, purple, and orange gown, a wide-brimmed hat in her hands.

"Now, where are you off to looking like a proper lady?" Missus Coleridge asked.

"I could ask you the same," I replied with a smile.

Outside, I heard the distinctive sound of a wagon. A horse whinnied then someone called, "Molly! Molly, let's go."

"Oh, I'm headed into the city to see my dead brother Rodger's second wife. She's remarried, but she always has time to see me. Clemeny! You should ride with us. Come on," she said.

Before I could protest, she grabbed me by the arm and hauled me out the front door. Closing up the place behind her, she pulled me toward a wagon. The driver eyed us both skeptically.

"You really shouldn't walk all dressed up as you are. No, no, it won't work having you getting all muddy. Ride with me in the carriage. Ephraim? Ephraim, this is Clemeny Louvel. We will take her across the bridge. She's one of my girls, a career woman. What is it you do again, Clemeny?"

Ephraim looked from Missus Coleridge to me. The expression on his face told me he couldn't care less.

"Law enforcement."

"Oh, you see, law enforcement. Isn't that interesting? Why don't we—"

"Both yous get in. I don't want to be late for my own affairs," the man interrupted.

Missus Coleridge climbed into the wagon, sliding across the bench to sit beside Ephraim who frowned when she got close.

"Ephraim is unattached, Clemeny. And he has a pig farm just outside the city."

That explained the smell. I looked into the back of the wagon. Under a tarp lay heaps of freshly slaughtered animals. I tried not to gag.

"Miss Louvel is also on the market," Missus Coleridge said, elbowing Ephraim.

To my horror, Ephraim paused a moment to look me over, seemingly considering if I might be a match. "That right?" he asked. His eyes raked my body with such intensity that I thought about stabbing him. But his gaze paused when he reached my face. "Down an eye, huh?"

"It's still there."

Ephraim nodded. "Same thing happened to my brother. Bull caught him with its horn. That horn scraped the eye clean out. Bloody mess."

"That's… I'm sorry to hear it," I said.

"I didn't know you had a brother," Missus Coleridge said. "And is he a bachelor as well?"

"He is, but he's out to sea. Miss Louvel, you in the market for a husband? You look like you're a strong enough girl."

Missus Coleridge clapped her hands excitedly.

Hell's bells. For years, Pastor Clark had been my one and only prospect. Now I was on my way to see my beau only to find myself being courted by a pig farmer while yet another man—well, werewolf—had expressed a strong desire to see me in a gown. What in God's name was happening?

"No, sir. Thank you."

Missus Coleridge sighed audibly. "Working women. No time for love. Unless, well… Off somewhere special, Clemeny?"

"Yes."

"Ooh," Missus Coleridge cooed excitedly. "Good for you! Sorry to get your hopes up, Ephraim."

"No harm done, Molly. No harm done."

I looked out at the Thames as we passed over the bridge. If the conversation lasted another minute, I was very certain I would have to throw myself into the river. But to my luck, Missus Coleridge began telling the pig farmer about Tilly, the seamstress who lived in the room across from mine. As we rode, Missus Coleridge doled out poor Tilly's entire life history, which Ephraim listened to with increasing interest. Poor Tilly.

The scent of decaying bacon, along with the rocking of the carriage, and the conversation, started pushing my limits. As soon as the wagon reached a section of the city where I knew I could find a society tram, I asked Ephraim to stop.

"Here?" Missus Coleridge asked. "But—"

"Oh, I'm meeting someone not far from here," I said as I scrambled quickly out of the wagon. "Enjoy your day, Missus Coleridge. Nice to meet you, Ephraim."

"You too, Miss Louvel," he said, tapping the brim of his straw cap.

Missus Coleridge waved to me, and they rode off.

Dipping into my satchel, I pulled out the tiny bottle of gardenia perfume I'd tossed in there who knows when. I liberally spritzed myself, hoping to shake the smell of rotting pig. Straightening my hat and smoothing down my skirt, I turned and headed in the direction of the entrance to the secret, underground tram.

Nervous butterflies fluttered through my stomach, but I tried to ignore them. This was going to be a good day. I had nothing to worry about. Quinn and Edwin were going to get along just fine. After all, my prospects were looking up. If things didn't work out with Edwin, there was always Ephraim to consider.

CHAPTER 10
It's a Date

Standing in front of Edwin's townhouse, I smoothed my skirt and adjusted my hat for the hundredth time. I suddenly wished I hadn't worn this stupid, fancy dress. I looked ridiculous. I felt ridiculous. This wasn't me. This was me pretending to be good enough to be on the arm of someone like Sir Edwin Hunter. My heart was thumping hard.

Oh, Clemeny, stop. It's just a bloody dress. I knocked on the door.

Edwin's butler opened the door, greeting me with a soft smile. "Agent Louvel, welcome. Agent Hunter was expecting you," he said. The man was considerably warmer than the last time I'd seen him.

I entered the townhouse. The last time I'd been here, we'd been hunting Krampus. I saw the place with new eyes this time. What if things did work out between Edwin and me? Then what? Would I live here, in this beautiful place? I eyed the pretty entryway with its hardwood floors, the rich cherry wood banister leading upstairs, the chandelier overhead, and the expensive paintings on the wall. Yes, that would do just fine.

"May I take your pelisse?" the footman asked.

I shook my head. "I expect we'll be leaving soon."

"Very well. I'll inform Sir Edwin that you're here. Would you like to adjourn to the parlor?"

"Sure."

The footman smiled and motioned for me to follow him.

Sir Edwin, son of the baronet. Strange that Edwin had never mentioned his father—nor his mother—in our talks. As I made my way to the parlor, I scanned the walls for family portraits but found none.

"Here you are, Agent Louvel," the man said, pushing open a set of double wooden doors, revealing a sunny room at the front of the house that looked out onto the street. The room had pretty furniture covered with pale pink and golden yellow fabric. There was a tall wicker birdcage in one corner. The little yellow bird therein called when I entered.

I crossed the room to look at the bird.

The tiny creature bounced from perch to perch, chirping at me. A moment later, I spotted a second head poke out of a basket hanging on the side of the cage. A decidedly sleepy bird looked out at his chirping friend.

"So, you work the night shift too?" I asked, grinning at the little creature.

"Finches," a voice said from behind me. "One brother is the talker. The other one sleeps as much as he can. Amusing little creatures."

I turned to find Edwin standing there, his top hat tucked under his arm. He was impeccably dressed in a grey suit and perfectly put together save a single lock of hair that had fallen onto his brow.

Joining him, I reached out gently and pushed the hair back in place. So close to him, I caught the scents of cinnamon and his shaving soap. Was that sandalwood? Perfection.

He smiled softly at me, that secret smile he shared on only rare occasions.

"You look very beautiful," he said.

"Looking pretty dapper yourself."

He chuckled then inclined his head to me. "Tram, carriage, horse, or steamauto?"

"Tram. Everything else takes too long."

"Very well," he said then put on his top hat.

We left the parlor to find the footman waiting. "Sir. Very nice to see you again, Agent Louvel."

"Thank you. You too."

Edwin smiled from the footman to me, a warm

knowing glance passing between him and his servant. With that, Edwin and I headed out. A well-dressed gentleman with a dainty lady on his arm, we were the perfect picture of manners…except one of us hunted werewolves and the other hunted demons.

CHAPTER 11
Rude Characters

We exited the tram and made our way down the sleepy Twickenham streets toward Quinn and Jessica's little house. As we went, Edwin adjusted his top hat and cravat about a hundred times.

"Everything all right?" I asked. I looked up at him.

Edwin cleared his throat, then cleared it again, then smiled down at me. "I never met Agent Briarwood formally, only spoke to him once or twice in passing. He has quite the reputation. Some say he was almost as fierce as you."

I chuckled. "You survived Grand-mère. Quinn shouldn't be as difficult."

"Shouldn't."

"Are you parsing words?"

"Indeed I am."

I squeezed his arm gently. It moved me to no end that Edwin wanted to make a good impression on the people I cared about most in the world.

Edwin slipped his hand over mine. "You know, there is a connection between the Rude Mechanicals and Twickenham," he said.

"I do believe you're changing the subject."

"Yes, I am."

"And you've caught me with something you know I want to hear. Carry on."

Edwin laughed. "Do you know of Strawberry Hill House?"

I nodded. "The Countess Waldegrave lives there."

"She is a story herself, but that house and land have long had ties to our benefactors. Mister Walpole, the man who built the house, was once attached to our society. He and Archibald Boatswain, the master tinker, have both been linked to the Rude Mechanicals."

"When I was working the *Fenrir* case, Lily Stargazer said something strange. She called *me* a Rude Mechanical. What do you think she meant by that?"

"It is all very secret, of course, but I believe that the Rude Mechanicals, the original order, used to do the job we do now."

"Marshaling the preternatural?"

"More or less."

"More or less?"

"Britannia has always been wild. At least there aren't as many mages as there used to be, and the faerie troupes intrude upon our world far less these days."

"That *would* be troublesome."

"And then there were the dragons."

I chuckled. "Dragons? Now you sound like a Pellinore," I said, referring to a quirky division in our agency dedicated to any leads related to dragons. Given there was no such thing, I imagined the three agents assigned to the job spent most of their time in the pub.

Edwin grinned. "Who knows what oddities live in our realm."

"Speaking of which, I have a lead on my case. Not to divert the conversation, but I was wondering if you'd be willing to take in the British Museum with me after lunch? Not only do they have a nice Assyrian exhibit going on, but a mark I'm after is going to be there."

"A werewolf at a museum? Unexpected."

"That it is. Though I don't know if he's a werewolf or not. Mr. Phillip Phillips, who is working with Alodie to cut some kind of deal, will be taking a tour of the museum. I need to get a look at him."

"Phillip Phillips? That's…unoriginal."

"That's what I thought."

Edwin eyed my dress. "You're a little light on weaponry."

I winked at him. "Don't let the gown fool you."

He chuckled. "I'd be happy to accompany you."

"You know a fight might break out at any time," I warned.

"Naturally. But that's the job."

"That it is."

We turned down the lane that led to Quinn and Jessica's house.

"Speaking of the job, if the Rude Mechanicals used to do our work, then I wonder who lorded over them, save the monarch, of course."

"That is an excellent question."

"And who are they now? I mean, Victoria directs us but who, exactly, are the Rude Mechanicals?"

"Also a good question. Have you ever watched Master Shakespeare's play *A Midsummer Night's Dream?*" Edwin asked.

I shook my head.

"In his play, a group of town citizens he calls the Rude Mechanicals find themselves mixed up in a marital squabble between the faerie king and queen."

"Do you think Master Shakespeare was one of us, er, them? A Rude Mechanical?"

"Perhaps. He knew of us, at least."

"Curious," I said.

Edwin nodded.

We had arrived at the small house where Quinn and Jessica lived. I looked up at Edwin. "Shall we?"

The corner of his mouth trembled. "All right."

I smiled to myself. I did feel a bit sorry for him, but the fact that he was nervous told me so much. Edwin actually cared about me.

CHAPTER 12
Tea, Lemonade, and Petit-Fours

Quinn's butler led us to the back of the house where Quinn and Jessica had a sunny garden patio.

Quinn, looking considerably relaxed but still too thin for my liking, rose to meet us. I couldn't help but notice he was using a cane to support himself.

His eyes must have followed mine because he said, "Nothing to worry about, partner. Just a pinch when I move around. Helps take the weight off."

"Ah, so that's where the weight has gone."

Quinn winked knowingly at me.

"Clemeny," Jessica said, embracing me and greeting me with a kiss on both cheeks.

"This is Agent Edwin Hunter," I said, turning to

Edwin who was standing in such a stiff, formal posture, his hat under his arm, that he looked like he might be made of stone.

Quinn reached out to shake his hand. "Sir," he said.

"It's a pleasure to meet you, Agent Briarwood," Edwin said with a polite bow. "I've heard many tales about your service to the realm."

"You hear that, Clem? I'm a legend now," Quinn told me.

"Of course you are," I replied, rolling my eyes.

"And Mrs. Briarwood," Edwin said, turning to Jessica.

She smiled at him. "A pleasure to meet you, Agent Hunter. Sit down. Both of you."

The garden had high stone walls that enclosed the space. It was a sunny spring day. The warmth of the sunshine fought off the chill of spring. A cherry blossom tree in one corner of the garden was covered in pale pink blossoms. Daffodils, hyacinth, tulips, and other spring flowers were growing in the flowerbeds nearby.

"Well, Clem, they land you with anyone yet?" Quinn said as he slowly lowered himself back into his chair.

I suppressed a frown at the sight. After all these months, he was still hurting. I chewed the inside of my cheek. Alodie was the one who had turned on Quinn. Now, look at him. I swallowed the anger that wanted to boil up in me. If I ever got ahold of that werewolf, she was going to pay for what she'd done.

"No, but Harper worked a case with me awhile back," I said.

"Harper," Quinn mused. "That little redhead?"

I nodded. "She's got some fire in her belly, just needs a bit of experience. She's on rotation though."

"Well, now that Agent Hunter has a personal interest in keeping you alive, I'm sure he'll find you someone," Quinn said then grinned at Edwin.

Edwin shifted in his seat. "Indeed. There have been some options, but I didn't think they were the right fit for Clemeny."

"Worked a case with Agent Rose this week. That was…messy."

Quinn laughed. "No doubt, no doubt," he said then looked at Jessica.

I followed his gaze. She was smiling wistfully at the cherry tree. Jessica never cared much for agent talk, and Quinn always tried to keep her out of it. I was not surprised when he then asked, "How is your grand-mère, Clem?"

"Remarkably quiet these days."

"Well done," Quinn told Edwin. "And you, Agent Hunter, what of your family?"

And so it begins. Moving deftly, Quinn turned the conversation into an interview.

"My father, Sir Edward Hunter, has retired to our estate in Antigua. He was previously attached to the crown as an attaché."

Quinn nodded. "And your mother?"

"She...she passed when I was a boy."

"I'm very sorry to hear that," Quinn said.

Jessica rose and set a comforting hand, albeit briefly, on Edwin's shoulder. "Let me go see about the refreshments. I had them make all your favorites, Clemeny," she said with a smile.

I looked at Edwin. I hadn't known anything about his mother. Most of our conversations had lingered around the job. I had sensed that there was something tender about his family issues, but I hadn't pressed. Now that the story was out, I was sorry for it.

Once Jessica left, Quinn turned to me. "So, what did Rose blow up this week?"

"It wasn't her. It was me. A fang exploded all over me. I didn't know they did that."

Quinn and Edwin both laughed.

"Yeah, I saw it happen once. Bloody awful," Quinn said.

"Literally," I replied with a laugh.

"Lionheart keeping things quiet for you?" Quinn asked.

A guilty pang crossed my heart, but I buried it. "Quiet enough, though some of the old pack is stirring up trouble. Edwin is going to help me follow up on a lead today."

"What kind of trouble?"

"I don't know, exactly. Alodie is mixed up in something. She's trying to leverage a way to bring back Cyril's old crew, and she's tracked down someone who was or is in the States. It has something to do with the American West. I don't know who or why yet."

Quinn grunted at the mention of Alodie's name. "Alodie. I don't know why Lionheart didn't just send her away. Can't you convince him, Clem? I always suspected he was partial to your charms."

I swallowed hard and glanced at Edwin out of the corner of my eye. My relationship with Lionheart was complicated and not one I wanted Edwin to be concerned with, but I could see from the expression on his face, that Edwin had caught Quinn's meaning.

"I need to know what she's after first. She got her hands on a shaman, used an elemental to track someone for her."

"Who?" Edwin asked.

I shook my head. "I don't know."

Quinn tapped his cane. "The American West... Do you remember Clara?"

"Clara?" I asked, trying to recall. The name was familiar, but I couldn't place her.

Quinn nodded. "She was Cyril's mate, though that

was long before you started the job. She and Cyril had a boy, but Cyril being Cyril, he was rough on the lad, so Clara took the pup and left. She went to the States. Arizona, I think. That must have been twenty or so years ago."

"Hell's bells. On the map, the shaman's monster conjured the image of a wolf wearing a crown."

"A prince," Edwin said.

"Dammit," I said with a frown. The packs would be unlikely to follow Alodie, but they would rally behind Cyril's blood. I needed to pluck that young wolf off the streets before anything got started. But first, I had to find him. I remembered then how the line on the map had twisted across America and the Atlantic. For all I knew, he could be here already. What was I doing making a social call when Alodie was about to usher in a war?

"Here we are. Tea, lemonade, and pastries. I have petit-fours and scones for you, Clemeny," Jessica said as a servant followed behind her pushing a cart. She paused and looked from Quinn to Edwin to me. "Well, I see I've stumbled into something."

"As usual, your husband just gave me a lead on a case," I said with a grateful nod to Quinn.

"We need to increase your retirement wages, Agent Briarwood," Edwin said good-naturedly.

Quinn grinned at him. "I like him, Clem."

At that, we all chuckled. Jessica fixed my tea precisely as I liked it and handed it to me.

"He's a good catch," she whispered, eyeing Edwin over her shoulder. "And you look so beautiful."

"Thank you," I said then looked her over. While Quinn was looking thin and gaunt, Jessica most certainly wasn't. In fact, being this close to her, I noticed that her heart-shaped face seemed far rounder, as did the rest of her. I gasped. Loudly.

Jessica laughed then turned to Quinn. "She finally noticed."

Quinn chuckled.

"A-are you?"

"Due in the autumn," Jessica said then touched her belly.

Setting my cup aside, I rose to embrace her. "Congratulations."

Jessica laughed lightly. "Thank you."

I went to my old partner then and took his hand, leaning in to kiss his cheeks. "Congratulations, my old friend," I whispered.

"Now, Clem. Don't get emotional. Between the dress and the beau, I'll barely recognize you."

I took him by his clean-shaved chin. "Could say the same for you. I'm so happy for you."

Quinn grinned at me.

"Wonderful news. Many felicitations," Edwin said, rising to shake Quinn's hand.

I winked at Quinn then turned and went to Edwin who looked down at me, giving me a brief, private smile. He set his hand on the small of my back.

Jessica lifted a plate of petit-fours and offered it to me. "Better take one now before I eat them all. There used to be twice as many. It was all I could do to save some for you," she said with a laugh.

Grinning, I gently pushed the plate back to her. "With my compliments to the little one," I said.

Edwin gently stroked my back. I look up at him once more. He reached out and lightly touched my chin, a sparkle in his eyes.

"How about some lemonade, Agent Hunter," Quinn said, barely suppressing the laugh in his voice.

Edwin gave me that slight smile once more then turned to Quinn. He coughed once then said, "Yes, please. Thank you," he said then went to the serving cart to get a drink.

Behind him, I gave Quinn a scolding look.

My old partner winked at me then turned to his wife. Jessica was pointing to all the sweets on the cart, describing them all to Edwin while she munched on petit-fours. Edwin gave Jessica a kind, friendly smile.

In that brief moment, all thoughts of Alodie and

Lionheart and werewolves vanished. Suddenly, I felt like I saw an image of the future.

And I loved it.

CHAPTER 13
Mister Phillip Phillips

We left Quinn and Jessica a few hours later and made our way back to the city in order to visit the British Museum.

Once we had turned the corner out of sight of Quinn and Jessica's house, Edwin exhaled a deep sigh of relief.

I chuckled. "As bad as that?"

He gave me a soft smile. "No, not at all. Mrs. Briarwood is lovely. It's just… Agent Briarwood is intimidating."

I laughed. "Intimidating? Haven't you faced some of the worst demons ever to pop up in our realm?"

"Yes, but none of them lorded in a fatherly manner over you. Do you… Do you think I did all right?"

"Edwin."

"I'm quite sincere, Clemeny. I really do want the people you care about to approve of our…match."

Our match. "Yes, you did all right."

Edwin smiled lightly. "Good. I've won over Agent Briarwood and your grand-mère. With those marks behind me, I think I'm all well and good to face your Mr. Phillips, whomever he is."

"That's the question, isn't it?"

Edwin nodded. "I haven't been to the museum since I was a boy. My mother used to take me on a tour from time to time. I must have been ten or so the last time I was there."

I had never actually been to the museum before but felt too embarrassed to say so. After all, the entry fee was not cheap, and Grand-mère only spent her money on necessities. But more, my thoughts went to Edwin and the small catch I'd heard in his voice when he spoke of his mother. "I'm sorry to hear about your mother."

Edwin nodded. "Thank you. It was a great loss. My father and I… Well, we never got along."

"And he's gone to Antigua?"

"We have an estate there. Victoria has given him some work to do on behalf of the crown. My father," Edwin said then paused, "made some embarrassing choices regarding a ward of his some years back. He left the country amongst scandal thereafter."

I raised an eyebrow at Edwin. "And the ward?"

"When she didn't get what she wanted, she left my father heartbroken and sauntered off to Italy in search of her next mark."

"I'm so sorry."

"We were lucky, in a way. My father figured out the game just in time. He left the family estate, Willowbrook Park, to me and took his eroded reputation into retirement with him."

"That must have been very difficult for you."

"It's no matter now. What about you, Clemeny? It's only you and your grand-mère?"

"The widow Louvel raised me. In truth, I have no idea who my real parents are. I was left as an orphan at Saint Clement Danes," I said, my stomach twisting with embarrassment.

"Any ideas about your birth family?"

I shook my head but then remembered Lionheart's words. I needed to go to the summer country. I debated for a moment on whether or not to tell Edwin. But tell him what? The preternaturals thought I smelled like roses. What did that even mean?

"It makes no difference. We shall carve our own paths forward," Edwin said.

I smiled up at him. "Sometimes literally."

He chuckled. "Indeed."

We took the tram from Twickenham to the British Museum, arriving about an hour before Phillip Phillips was scheduled for his tour. Checking in with the guards —who eyed Edwin and me suspiciously—to alert them to our presence and possible complications, they permitted us to carry on. The massive museum had been under construction for many years, only reopening of late. Edwin and I headed toward the Assyrian exhibit.

"Who do we have working in the thieves' colony watching my old boys?" I asked Edwin as we wove between the massive, ancient stone sculptures.

Edwin frowned. "Not the Clemeny Louvel of Australia, I'm afraid. Some good field agents, but, it seems, not good enough.

I paused in front of a statue of a winged lion with the head of a man.

"From the royal palace in Nimrud. Related to the war goddess Ishtar," Edwin read from a plaque.

I looked up at the tall sculpture which was more than double my height. It occurred to me then that not only had the preternaturals roamed our own realm for hundreds of years, but they had done so worldwide for millennia in a variety of forms.

"The fighting lion was a symbol of the war goddess," Edwin continued.

I studied the statue. The man's head was armored.

Did they have shape-shifting lions in ancient Assyria? Suddenly I was glad I was only hunting wolves.

We moved from the statues to study the reliefs that had come from the walls of ancient temples. On them, I saw massive ships, depictions of war, gods and goddesses, and more lions.

"When I faced Skollson, Lionheart warned me that wolf culture was deeply ingrained in Norwegian myth because the preternaturals nearly outnumbered the humans at one point. Do you suppose it was like that in other cultures?" I asked, my fingertips just touching the image of a man-lion.

Edwin considered the relief. "We may tease our Pellinore brothers and their endless and seemingly futile dragon hunts, but there is a reason King Arthur was called a Pendragon."

I scoffed. "You can't be serious. Dragons?"

Edwin raised a playful eyebrow at me then turned back to the figure. "Just be glad you don't have to worry about dragons. Besides, your wolves keep you busy enough. It's good that Sir Richard is inclined to speak to you. Agent Greystock informed me that his cooperation is not easily won."

There was an undertone to his voice that I didn't miss. Suspicion? Jealousy? I was probably reading more into it than I should. "He's too smart and too crafty for any of our good, but he's loyal to the crown.

He just needs to be firmly reminded of it from time to time."

Edwin nodded, but I noticed his stance was a bit stiffer than it had been a moment before.

It was then that the palms of my hands and bottoms of my feet started to prickle. I motioned to Edwin.

"Someone's here," I whispered.

Nodding, Edwin took my hand, and we found a discreet spot away from the crowd behind a statue of the goddess Astarte. The room was brimming with people. I scanned the gallery. Someone was here. Who? Where?

Edwin pulled out the small device he had used on the Krampus case. Adjusting a nob thereon, he scanned the room. To my surprise, the device sparked to life, glowing and beeping intensely.

Edwin frowned.

"What is it?" I asked.

"The relics are charged. They're throwing things off."

"The relics are charged?" I asked, looking up at the statue of the ancient goddess.

The statue of the goddess Astarte had wide, round hips, her hands cupping her breasts which had been covered loosely by a swath of fabric. She had a placid look on her face and wore a crescent moon on her head. I closed my good eye and glanced at the statue with my mooneye. There was something there, just below the surface, like a wave of heat coming off the figure.

But then, I heard a laugh I couldn't miss.

I sighed.

Edwin looked at me. "What is it?"

I frowned. "Alodie," I whispered almost inaudibly.

Making sure the veil I was wearing fully covered my face, I looked around the statue and followed the sound of the ultra-feminine laughter. There I found Alodie on the arm of the gentleman she'd visited the night before. He was pointing at a relief of King Gilgamesh. Alodie, who was impeccably dressed in a lemon-colored gown with lace trim, carrying a pretty parasol, clung to his every word.

"Dammit," Edwin said, unbuttoning his jacket and pulling out his gun.

"What is it?"

"I don't know what's going on, but I do know who he is."

"Him?" I asked. "Phillip Phillips?"

Edwin nodded. "Yes, Phillip Phillips. Of course, that is not his real name. His name is Rumpole, and he is a demon."

At the sound of his name, the small man turned and looked across the room toward us. His eyes flashed brightly for just a moment, and the expression on his face darkened.

Alodie, who was still giving the man a fake laugh, patting his arm as she did so, noticed her mark was distracted. Following his gaze, she turned and looked at us. Her eyes narrowed as she looked me over. Fury washed over her face as she realized it was me. She shook her head angrily, her jaw clenching.

But at that moment, it wasn't her I was worried about. Whomever Rumpole was, he recognized Edwin, and that terrible creature was about to unleash hell.

CHAPTER 14
Ishtar Rises

"Hell's bells," I whispered, pulling my pistol from my boot.

"Clemeny," Edwin said warningly.

But he didn't have to say a word. The shutters on the tall windows of the gallery slammed shut, and the lights above flickered out. A torrent of wind began to circle the room.

The human tourists, shocked and frightened by this sudden and inexplicable weather occurrence in the middle of their casual museum viewing, hurried for the doors, which was a good thing. Phillip Phillips was about to come unglued from his mild-mannered disguise.

A fact about which even Alodie looked surprised.

"What the hell?" Alodie said, stepping back as she looked at the man.

"Stupid wolf," Phillip Phillips said in a voice that echoed throughout the chamber. He flung out a hand toward her, sending Alodie flying across the room.

"Bloody hell," I said then pulled my knife.

The doors to the gallery slammed closed as the wind picked up.

"Edwin Hunter," the demon called, walking slowly toward him.

One of the museum guards raced into the room, his gun drawn.

"What's happening here?" the man demanded.

The demon lifted his hand. A strange black smoke emanated from his fingers, lashing out like a sword that plunged into the man's chest. A spray of blood blasted all over the statue from the temple of Ishtar. My mooneye saw the figure tremble, the head turning in the direction of the demon.

Edwin dipped into his pocket and pulled out a tinkered device. He advanced on the demon as he began speaking loudly in Latin.

Phillip Phillips—Rumpole—twitched violently. "Silence," the demon commanded then reached toward Edwin, black smoke teetering on his fingertips.

"Oh no you don't," I said then took aim and fired.

The shot hit home, the bullet slamming through the demon's chest. He paused a moment, turning as if someone had tapped him on the shoulder, and looked at me.

He flung his hand toward me.

I gasped.

"No," Edwin shouted.

Alodie laughed.

I stared, frozen, as the strange snaky smoke came hurdling at me. But then, something inside of me sparked to life. It was like a light flickered on inside me.

I raised my hand. "No."

The smoke stopped, recoiling like it had run against something, stopping when it came near.

Edwin activated the device in his hand. The machine shot small, wooden darts at the demon who staggered backward upon impact. Once again, Edwin began chanting, working to exorcise the demon.

"You won't escape this time, Rumpole. And now I'm twice as motivated to vanquish you," he said, casting an anxious glance toward me.

Alodie was staring wide-eyed at the scene. But realizing this was her moment, she began to sneak toward the exit.

My gun trained on the demon, I debated what to do.

"Edwin," I called, motioning to the escaping werewolf.

He tilted his head toward the door, indicating that it

was okay for me to leave, as he crossed the room toward Phillip Phillips...or instead, what was left of Phillip Phillips. The guise of the little man was melting off the body of the demon. Edwin continued his incantation.

Yanking on the door handle, Alodie turned and raced out.

Cursing my stupid dress, I dashed after her.

Alodie raced down the narrow gallery, pausing to glance back over her shoulder at me. Seeing me hustling behind her, she picked up her step.

A fleet of guards passed us as they rushed toward the Assyrian gallery.

They were in for a terrible surprise.

Alodie slipped through the crowd in the portrait gallery and pushed open a side door. I rushed along behind her, blasting outside. The moment I did so, however, something bashed me in the head. Jarring sideways, I turned to see Alodie standing there, brandishing her parasol in front of her.

"Really, Alodie? A parasol?" I said, giving her a snide look. I didn't want her to know it, but I was kind of impressed. That parasol had hurt.

She glared at me.

Slipping my hand into my pocket as I regained my footing, I slid on the silver knucklebuster hidden there.

BITCHES AND BRAWLERS

Alodie swiped at me again. I ducked then turned, catching her with a jab to the stomach.

Moving back, she swung her parasol again. I grabbed it, tugged her toward me, then gave her a swift kick to the stomach.

Alodie dropped the parasol and stepped back. She glanced behind her, looking like she was about to run.

I righted myself then punched Alodie squarely in the face.

I could hear the sizzle as the silver knucklebuster connected with her skin.

She screamed and stepped back, her hand on her cheek.

"Little Red," she hissed at me. "You're going to pay for this—you, Lionheart, and that Agent Hunter."

"Consorting with demons. Could you go no lower?"

"Do you think I knew he was a demon?"

"Then you're sneaky *and* stupid."

Alodie lunged at me, but I caught her with a right uppercut.

A moment later, however, I heard gunfire, and a bullet whizzed past my ear.

I turned to find two of Alodie's bitches, both with weapons trained on me.

Alodie glared at me. "This isn't over, Louvel," she said with a growl, her eyes flashing red.

"You're right. It isn't over until you pay for what you did to Quinn."

Her hand still pressed against her cheek, she turned and ran toward her pack.

I thought about following, shooting, or causing more mayhem, but the sky above the museum was twisting and turning black like a tornado had suddenly appeared in the middle of London. Given Alodie's girls had their weapons on me, it was time to go.

I flung open the museum door and ran back inside.

I raced to the hall where I'd left Edwin. The guards who'd gone rushing past me were nowhere to be seen. I yanked on the handle to the gallery, but the door was firmly shut.

Inside, I heard Edwin's voice chanting loudly in Latin. Along with that, I heard the strange hissing voice of Phillip Phillips who was trying to avoid being vanquished.

But below them both, I heard another voice. A deep female voice called out to me.

Clemeny, come. Warrior, come.

The door clicked then slowly swung open.

The first thing I saw—well, with my mooneye—was the flashing obsidian eyes of the fighting lion statue as it turned and looked down at me.

I stared at the statue, the living, breathing statue,

alive only with the sight of my mooneye. The creature inclined its head toward me.

The demon howled then cursed in a language I didn't understand. Looking away from the statue, I turned to Edwin and the beast.

A pile of flesh and clothing lay on the floor where Phillip Phillips used to be. The nearly ethereal form of the demon Rumpole stood there. He had horns, a long tail, and bright yellow eyes.

The wind blew wildly. The whole place was engulfed in a tempest.

Shouting loudly, a look of determination on his face, Edwin spoke the final word of his incantation.

Rumpole froze. Then, he exploded.

Gobs of ashy goo flung around the room splattering everything, including me. Edwin, who'd been ready for it, had turned his back. Me, on the other hand, stood there covered in a splatter of demon.

"Hell's bells!"

"Clemeny," Edwin called.

As I wiped the glop off my face, I heard the sound of crying and whimpering. The guards who'd rushed past me were huddled at the base of the lion of Ishtar. I looked up at the statue which seemed to tremor once more, a smile on its face, then the effigy became still.

Edwin, who was shaking some slime off his hand,

crossed the room toward me. Pulling a handkerchief from his pocket, he handed it to me.

"This isn't your week," he said.

"That is an understatement."

"Alodie?"

"Outgunned. I let her go." I looked at the body of the guard who lay dead on the floor. I shook my head. Such a senseless death. Alodie had a lot to answer for.

"I've been chasing Rumpole for years. He slipped me in Portugal, and I wasn't able to track him after that. I never would have guessed Australia. What was he doing with the wolves?"

"No idea, but I don't think Alodie knew he was a demon. Or she's lying. Either is probable."

"Well, looks like we both have a mess to clean up. I'll contact the agency. You…oh, my dear," he said then shook his head. "You are a mess, Clemeny Louvel."

"That I am. I'll go to Grand-mère's."

Edwin chuckled. "Are you sure?"

I sighed. First, bursting pipes, then an exploding fang, and now this? What was next? I was suddenly glad werewolves only quadrupled in strength and got considerably hairier when they were at full power.

Edwin grinned at me. "I'd kiss you, but, well, you know."

I smirked. With my cleanish hand, I took his hand and give it a squeeze. "See you soon."

Turning, I headed out of the museum, well aware of what a spectacle I was. But at least the world was down one demon. Now I needed to reduce the werewolf numbers by one.

Right after a bath.

CHAPTER 15
What Grand-mère Knew

Bracing myself, I knocked on Grand-mère's door.

"Grand-mère?"

"Oh, Clemeny, oranges and lemons, my Clemeny," I heard Grand-mère call as she undid the locks. The door swung open, Grand-mère fully ready to embrace me, but then she stopped.

"*What* is that?" she asked.

"*Who* is more correct."

Grand-mère started cursing in French then stepped back so I could enter. Still muttering, she headed to the kitchen. "Go get that dress off. I'll bring the hot water."

"Thank you, Grand-mère."

"Oh, Clemeny."

"At least it's not blood."

Grand-mère huffed. "As if whatever—whomever —*that* makes it any better. Your dress!"

"I have another one."

"Yes, but *one* other. I'd swear you're trying to ruin them on purpose. I hope, at least, that Edwin got to see you before you were covered in this mess."

"It's Edwin's fault that I'm covered in this mess."

Grand-mère cursed in French once more.

I chuckled. "Remind yourself, Grand-mère, that he is *Sir* Edwin Hunter. And from what I've learned, apparently he has a nice country estate somewhere," I said, trying to give Grand-mère something else to worry herself with besides the state of my clothing.

"What? Where? What is it called?"

"Willowbrook Park."

"Oh, my Clemeny, that sounds very fine. Yes, that will do perfectly. Has he proposed yet?"

In my tiny room in the flat, I began pulling off my spoiled dress. God, the smell was something else. The dress would need to be burned. I laughed. "No, Grand-mère."

"Well, you must try to hurry him along. You need to show a little more skin, my girl. Entice him. Give him some motivation."

"Grand-mère!" I said, scandalized and amused all at once.

I glanced down at my undergarments, which could certainly use an upgrade if I was going to impress a man. But Grand-mère was wrong. I didn't need to show off anything to win Edwin. That was why I adored him. To my great fortune, Edwin liked me the way I was.

Grand-mère entered with a basin of soapy water. She clicked her tongue disapprovingly at me. "You're skin and bones."

"You always say that."

"You've always been skin and bones."

"And muscle."

Grand-mère clicked her tongue again. "If you had married Pastor Clark, you'd be plump and with child by now. Instead, God only knows what trouble you've gotten yourself into."

"But then I wouldn't have Willowbrook Park in my line of sight, would I? I saw Jessica and Quinn this morning. They are expecting a child."

Grand-mère pulled out a stool and sat me down. At once, she began washing my hair. "I'd thought Quinn a bit beyond his years for that."

"Is a man ever beyond his years for that?"

Grand-mère chuckled. "No. You're right."

I grinned. "Jessica was absolutely radiating."

"As all women do when they are carrying the child of a man they love. You, too, will be like that one day."

I scrunched up my brow. I had never considered myself a motherly type. And the fact that I didn't know who I was, or where I came from, always made me feel I had no business with a child. When I'd encountered

Marlowe, that strange light inside me had sparked to life and saved me from being thrown off an airship. Today, it had saved me from a demon.

"Who is your family?" Lionheart had asked me. The memory of his question bonged through my mind once again. I didn't know. I had no idea why I was like this or what this even was.

"Grand-mère," I began carefully. "Was there—I was just wondering—was there ever any indication of where I came from? Did anyone ever come around looking for me? Any…hint?"

My grand-mère, who was rubbing soapy water into my hair, paused.

I didn't want to hurt her with the question. She was everything to me. But still.

"When we found you? No. Nothing. When you were a girl, though, a woman once came to the church for service. Her eyes never left you. But she left when the service ended and never spoke a word to anyone."

I frowned. "Maybe she just liked children."

Grand-mère was silent.

"Grand-mère?"

"She had long, black hair and a steely gaze like someone else I know. When I finished the last song for the sermon, I came downstairs to find her, but she was gone."

"You…you never told me before."

"What is there to tell? Maybe it was only a coincidence."

"But it was odd enough that it got your attention."

"Why do you ask, my girl?" Grand-mère began washing my hair once more.

"I just… Sometimes I feel like there is something different about me."

"Of course, there is no more special girl in the world."

"No, Grand-mère. There is just something…different. That same something different that made Eliza Greystock notice me."

"Eliza saw you were sharp-witted, that's all."

I frowned. I realized then that even if Grand-mère knew precisely what I was talking about, she'd never admit it.

"I'm sorry to ask. I hope you know I would never replace you with anyone. I was just—"

"Curious. It's only natural. Especially if you are dreaming of a family of your own. With Edwin. At Willowbrook Park. Where I will come and live with you."

I chuckled. "Of course you will."

Grand-mère patted my shoulder but stayed remarkably silent thereafter as she worked her rose-scented soap through my hair, washing the last of Phillip Phillips away.

"I love you, Grand-mère."

"I love you too, my Clemeny."

CHAPTER 16
Rattled

Fully scrubbed, redressed, and smelling like someone who hadn't been covered in demon goo an hour ago, I thanked Grand-mère profusely then headed back out on the job.

It was already late afternoon, which meant the sun was going to go down soon. The situation with Alodie was beginning to get unwieldy. If I was going to try to go toe-to-toe with Alodie again, I was going to need help.

I turned and headed toward Temple Square. I was surprised when my Templar brothers, upon seeing me approach, simply opened the gate. I recognized one of the guards.

"Sir Handel," I said, nodding to him. So close to nightfall, it didn't escape my notice that he had a fiery red glint in his eyes.

He inclined his head to me. "Agent Louvel. Lionheart is in the chapel."

"Thank you," I said then entered the square, fully aware that they closed and locked the gate behind me.

The palms of my hands prickled. Was it possible Lionheart was in on all this mess? Or the Templars? Was I walking into a trap?

Shut it, Clemeny. Remember who they are.

I berated myself for my paranoia and headed toward the chapel. My hands were itching because I was walking into pack territory, no more.

As quietly as possible, I opened the door of the chapel and entered. I crossed the marble floor of the rotunda where the shrines were located. At the altar at the front of the chapel, I spotted Lionheart who was kneeling in prayer, his sword poised hilt up, taking on the shape of the cross, before him.

I paused.

He would know it was me. I didn't have to say anything. I leaned against one of the tall columns and considered him.

It moved me that he still mourned the family lost so long ago. There was fierce love and loyalty in that. That his care extended to Bryony told me more about the quality of the man below the lupine infection. A knight. A widower. A pious man. A scholar. Pity he was a werewolf. Really, really a pity.

Lionheart whispered the final words of his prayer, ending with an *amen*, then rose. He made the sign of the cross, belted his sword, and turned to join me.

"There is a rumor among the packs that you have some mystical power. No one can understand how they always miss your skulking. They never hear you coming, never even sense you."

"And what about you?"

"I knew it was you."

"How?"

"Red roses...and gardenia," he said with a smirk.

I rolled my eyes. "I thought being in here pained you."

"It does. Well, out with it, Agent Louvel. I can see it on your face that something has happened."

"Alodie. I believe she's rallying the troops and trying to crown a new alpha."

"Who?" Lionheart asked in a low growl.

"Cyril's son, if my hunch is right."

Lionheart clenched his jaw. "Cyril's son. Is he here?"

I shook my head. "I don't know. She's been working with an Australian merchant to bring the old pack back to London. Of course, he wasn't really a merchant. He was a demon posing as a merchant."

"A demon? Which one?"

"Rumpole."

Lionheart frowned.

"He's—I think I scraped the last of him off the bottom of my boot a bit back—he's not to be worried about. Alodie was just using him, or so she thought, to get Cyril's dogs back into the realm. I don't think she even knew he was a demon. Actually, I'm not sure who was using whom. Either way, she has the wolves all worked up with the idea of reuniting the old pack under Cyril's boy. She seems rather hell-bent on revenge on us both."

Lionheart puffed air through his lips. "You were right. I should have banished her."

"I know," I replied with a wink.

Lionheart rolled his eyes at me then motioned to the door. Taking his lead, we headed outside. The dusk sky was fading into indigo, purple, and orange colors.

"The boy's name is Cole. I remember the gossip when Clara left. It's a smart move on Alodie's part. He would be of age, and young, and strong," Lionheart said.

"But he's no Templar."

"No," Lionheart said with a soft smile, but a noise caught his attention, and he turned in the direction of one of the buildings surrounding the square. To my surprise, I saw Bryony there. Carrying a case, she walked toward us.

"Clemeny," she called warmly, waving to me.

I raised an eyebrow at Lionheart.

"She can't stay in the city with Alodie stirring up trouble, and she can't stay here either. I'm sending her to the country for a time," he explained in a low breath.

"Send someone with her."

Lionheart nodded. "Sir Geoffrey will accompany her."

Bryony nodded to Lionheart. "I'm ready. Sir Geoffrey is coming along now. Just one more stop then I'll be on my way."

"Stop?" Lionheart asked.

She nodded. "I forgot my journal at my flat."

"Please, don't delay."

"Trust me. I have no wish to see those people ever again. But it is good to see you, Clemeny. Why is it that whenever danger is in abundance, you are not far behind?" she asked.

"Just luck."

"I'd wish that luck on no one."

I chuckled.

A burly werewolf crossed the commons toward us. "Sir," he said, giving Lionheart a courteous bow. He eyed me over then inclined his head to me.

"Sir Geoffrey. Do you have everything you need?" Lionheart asked him.

"Yes, sir."

Lionheart looked at Bryony. Sir Geoffrey and I, both taking the cue, stepped away. But my curiosity tugged at me. I glanced at the pair out of the corner of my eye. There was tenderness between them. Bryony clearly loved him, but did he love her? I could see he cared for her. But did he love her? I just didn't see the spark. Or maybe that was my jealousy talking.

Sighing, I looked away. I scanned the complex. As I looked around, I noticed that the wolves here were very busy. Usually, the place was sedate. Tonight, the pack was on the move. What were they up to?

With a few low words, Lionheart wished Bryony safe travels.

No kiss.

"Bye, Clemeny. Be safe," she said with a smile as she and Sir Geoffrey passed. She set her hand on my shoulder and leaned into my ear. "Watch over him for me."

Grinning, I nodded to her. "Of course." I cast a glance over my shoulder at Lionheart who was smirking. I winked at him.

Bryony and Sir Geoffrey passed through the gates. A few moments later, a steamauto outside sparked to life, and the pair drove off.

"You have a plan, I assume?" Lionheart said.

"We need to track Alodie. The Templars should round up the stray dogs in the dark district. And when I say round up, let's just go ahead and end their miserable lives, shall we? Seems like that might send a stronger message."

"That was my plan as well. As you see, the Templars are getting ready as we speak," he said, motioning to the square. "Blackwood will lead the assault on the dark district."

"If you already had a plan, then why ask me?"

"I wanted to see if we were in agreement."

"And how did you know I'd even come by?"

Lionheart gave me that wolfy grin but said nothing.

I frowned, not so much at him, but at the stupid butterflies swarming in my stomach. I envisioned taking out my pistol and shooting them all, but no matter what—even in my own imagination—I kept missing.

"Well, shall we?" Lionheart asked.

"I suppose you want to rattle me around on that bike of yours again."

"I wouldn't pass up the opportunity to rattle you around for anything in the world, Agent Louvel."

"Your girlfriend just left. Stop flirting with me."

"Who's flirting?"

I shook my head. "Fine. Let's go."

CHAPTER 17
Absolutely Maybe

"I also had eyes on Alodie. We saw she was stirring up trouble, but it was unclear of what nature besides recruiting Cyril's old dogs. We spotted Antoinette and a henchman this morning and had them followed. I have a lead on where to look," Lionheart said as he pulled on his cycle goggles. He handed a pair to me, pausing to look at me for a moment. "You stopped wearing the eyepatch."

"It was unbalancing me," I said in something of a lie. The truth was, the mooneye's sight was an unexpected gift. As it had in the Assyrian exhibit, it saw things my other eye could not see. Why or how was still beyond me, but I liked it.

Lionheart nodded, but his expression told me he didn't fully believe my words. Annoying, perceptive werewolf.

I slipped on the goggles. "Who?"

"Who?"

"Whose eyes have you had on Alodie? I haven't seen any Templars in the dark district."

"No. Alodie would have easily noted them. I employed the aid of a friendly witch."

"A witch?"

"Yes."

"My, you have friends in the oddest places, don't you?"

"Oh, Agent Louvel, you have no idea. Hop on," he said, motioning behind him.

I slid onto the seat behind him and wrapped my arms around him. Every inch of my body was tingling. He was so warm. And he felt…more right than he should.

"Why, Agent Louvel—"

"Shut it."

"You want to drive?"

"No."

"Why, can't you drive?"

"Of course I can drive. I just don't want to. Can we go now, please?"

Chuckling, Lionheart sparked the steamcycle to life with a hiss, and we set off on our way.

To my surprise, Lionheart drove, not toward the dark district, but toward the docks.

"Why are we going this way?"

"Antoinette was seen talking to the harbormaster this morning. I sent someone around behind them with enough money to get people to talk. And they did."

"And what did they say?"

"To expect a ship tonight. I just didn't know who or what would be on that ship. I expected more werewolves, not Cyril's boy."

"Well, let's see if London's prodigal son is making a return."

And if he was, things were about to get very complicated.

We drove toward the busy Thames hub then made our way to the dock where the ship was expected to make port. The traffic at the London shipyard was hectic. Everywhere we went, sailors rushed back and forth. Carts were loaded with goods from ships. Even this late in the day, the shipyard was packed. The briny scent of the river and the stink of fish filled the air, making my nose wrinkle and my stomach protest.

Lionheart pulled out his pocket watch. "We may have a wait, Agent Louvel."

"If the ship is coming from the Americas, there is no way they can know when it will arrive."

"It isn't coming from the Americas. Alodie's girl was inquiring about a ship coming in from Calais."

"Calais?"

Lionheart nodded.

I frowned, annoyed with myself. I had anticipated an airship from the Americas, not a schooner from Calais. Alodie was using the back door, of course.

"Come on," Lionheart said, motioning for me to follow as he headed in the direction of a trashy looking pub.

"There?"

"An ale to pass the time."

When we entered the pub, a few people looked up and inspected us. Given I was without my red cape—it was still at Missus Coleridge's with Fenton—I didn't bring undue attention. The place stunk of ale and fish. Lionheart and I headed to a table near a window through which we had a good view of the dock.

We slipped into our seats, Lionheart waving to the tapster who sent a lad no more than nine years old over with two mugs of ale.

"Want food?" the boy asked.

I grinned at him, remembering the little street rats I'd encountered at Christmas.

"No, lad," Lionheart said, patting the boy on the head.

My heart melted…just a little.

The boy left the drinks then went back to work.

Lionheart lifted his mug. "God save the Queen."

BITCHES AND BRAWLERS

"God save the Queen," I echoed, clicking my mug against his.

I lifted the ale and glanced out the window. Reminding myself to drink slowly this time, not wanting a repeat of the shenanigans in Edinburgh, I took just a sip and set the tankard back down.

I looked back at Lionheart whose eyes were still on the boy.

"My son was about that age," he said then took another drink of the brew.

I stared at Lionheart. He was far more unsettled than I'd ever seen him before. Bryony's influence had shaken the knight, reminded him of a past he'd buried. Now, the ghosts of the man he had been lingered around him. And it was unbalancing him just when he needed to be his sharpest.

I looked back at the boy who was busy wiping down tables. The child, dressed in knee-length pants, a vest, oversized shirt, and boots with no laces, was a slim lad with dark hair and a face full of freckles.

Part of me was dying with curiosity about Lionheart's past. The other part of me wanted to shake him hard, snap him out of it, and force him to get his head on straight before he got himself killed. Curiosity won out. "What was his name?" I asked.

Lionheart smiled softly. "Harry," he said, but then his smile faded. He shook his head. "It's been so long, I can barely remember his face," he said then took another drink.

"I... I'm sorry."

Lionheart drank again then slid back into his seat and gazed at me. "And how was your outing?"

"Interrupted by wolf hunting and demon vanquishing."

"Unfortunate. And you never did say with whom you went."

"No, I did not."

"Must be someone from the society."

"And why do you say that?"

"It will be hard for you to find someone who can understand you. It would need to be another agent."

I raised an eyebrow at him. "Really? Are you an expert now that you're in love?"

"Who said I'm in love?"

A sound like an alarm began wailing in my head. "I just assumed."

He drank again. "She loves me. I care for her, and I don't want her to die just because she fell in love with me," he said then looked out the window.

A flurry of thoughts spun through my mind, most of them echoing sentiments of relief, which just made me angry at myself.

"Sir Edwin Hunter," I spat out.

Lionheart raised an eyebrow at me. "Your boss?"

"Yes."

He tapped his finger on his lips as he considered. Arching his eyebrows, he shrugged then polished off his mug.

"What, no comment?" I said.

"Yes. I need another drink."

"You're not yourself, Sir Richard."

He winked at me. "Who else would I be?"

He waved to the tapster who sent over another ale. I sat back in my seat and eyed the room. Drunken sailors, pickpockets, fishermen, and a few tarty girls filled the place, but there was no one out of the ordinary that I could detect.

"Scanning for mermaids?" Lionheart asked.

"There is no such thing as mermaids."

"Really, Louvel. I'd think you know better by now."

"Right then. I'm watching for mermaids riding unicorns."

"Now you're being ridiculous. Of course, there's no such thing as unicorns."

I chuckled then glanced out the window.

"Speaking of peculiarities, have you ever followed up with the druids?" Lionheart asked.

"Peculiarities? Are *you* calling *me* peculiar, Sir Richard?"

"I am indeed."

"No, I have not followed up with the druids."

He nodded slowly as he looked carefully at me, his eyes lingering on mine. My mooneye focusing on him, I saw the oddest shape around him, seeing him and the silhouette of the wolf all at once.

He lifted his mug. "I have," he said, taking a sip.

I set my drink down. "You have what?"

"I have made inquiries. You know, we Templars have many old texts. If one is curious, inclined to research, fat with coin, and determined, it isn't hard to turn over a few stones, even if they are ring-shaped menhir. And I am, of course, a curious creature. Why does this slip of a woman I know have a spine of steel and smell like roses? It puzzled me. I don't like being puzzled."

I stared at him. My heart pounded in my chest. "And?"

Lionheart reached into his pocket and pulled out a piece of paper. He slid it across the table toward me.

I gazed at the paper, overcome with the distinct feeling that it might burn me.

"A name and address. There are answers for you in the summer country. I couldn't find exactly what I was looking for, and the Dís wouldn't wake up. But this is a start."

"You went to the Dís? For me?"

Lionheart shrugged.

Willing my hand not to tremble, I pulled the paper

toward me. Unfolding it, I found a name and address in Cornwall written in Lionheart's eloquent hand. "Evelyn Dulac. Who is she?"

"A druid priestess."

"I… Thank you."

He winked at me then sipped his ale again. His eyes went back to the boy who sat on a stool in the corner playing with a paddleball.

I stared at Lionheart. He'd gone looking for an answer for me. His gesture moved me more than I cared to admit. And he didn't love Bryony. Was it possible… Could he possibly… Could I… No. Not only was it impossible for a person like me to be attached to a person like Lionheart, but there was also Edwin. And the truth was, I was falling in love with Edwin.

Turning, I looked back out the window. I had always fancied that the attraction between Lionheart and me was just physical, playful. Was it possible Lionheart actually cared for me? No. I couldn't let whatever was trying to bloom between us to see the light of day.

"Agent Louvel," Lionheart began, his voice soft.

As I stared at the window and tried not to feel anything for Lionheart, I noticed that a ship was slowly making its way toward the dock. It was the vessel from Calais.

"Our ship has come in," I said.

Lionheart paused. "Sorry?"

I pointed out the window then pulled some coins from my vest and set them on the table. I flicked my eyes toward Lionheart and for a moment, saw a tender expression on his face. In truth, that gaze terrified me. It called forth a pool of emotion I had no business swimming in.

Hell's bells. No way, Clemeny.

"The vessel is here," I said then polished off my drink. "Shall we go crack some skulls?"

At that, Lionheart chuckled. "After you."

CHAPTER 18

The Prince

Lionheart and I slipped out of the tavern and headed down the dock. As we moved, we stayed in the shadows. I scanned the deck of the ship. Thus far, I only spotted human passengers. But I could feel the energy of someone, or several someones, nearby.

Casting a glance up at the moon, I clenched my jaw then checked my pistols once more. Hunting wolves during the day was one thing. Hunting them at night when they could shift form was something altogether different.

Once the ship tied in, one of the sailors headed belowdecks. Not long after, two Lolitas, three of Cyril's old boys, and a young man about my age with a head of shaggy red hair emerged. The redhead was massive, towering over the others. The werewolves headed down the plank toward the dock.

I cast a glance at Lionheart. "Sure you don't want to get Blackwood?"

"Why do I need Blackwood? I have you," he said with a wink. Motioning to me, we headed in.

⓪

THE BYLAWS OF THE RED CAPE SOCIETY SUGGEST THAT WE do our work in secret, that London's residents don't get an eyeful of anything strange, and that we avoid public mayhem. While I'm sure those bylaws work very well for the magical artifacts division, they don't work for my beat.

No sooner had Lionheart and I stepped out of the darkness than one of the Lolita's caught wind of the alpha.

"Trouble," I heard her say as she pulled her pistol.

But she was already too late.

Jumping up on a stack of crates, I took aim and got off a shot, downing the werewolf before she had a chance to kick up a fuss. Her sister wolf looked in my direction.

"Little Red," she snarled.

But no sooner had she spoken the word when Lionheart—in fully shifted form—blasted from behind the stack of boxes.

Hesitating, I stared. He had shapeshifted when my back was turned. While it was not the first time I saw him like this, the sight took me aback. More wolf than man now, with a long maw full of sharp teeth, clawlike hands, and a massive muscular body, he jumped, crossing the dock in one powerful leap.

Two of Cyril's old dogs turned to face him while the other Lolita and one of the werewolves, a former member of Paddington pack, led Cyril's pup away.

Taking aim, I shot at the Paddington werewolf.

"Kill her," the Lolita yelled, pointing at me as she rushed away, Cole in tow.

Shifting form, the werewolf leaped toward me.

I pulled my knife and waited for him to get close.

The wolf leaped up, trying to swipe me off the stack of boxes, but I jumped, leaving the wolf to tumble on the crates.

Shaking his head, he struggled to right himself. As he did so, I rushed up from behind and plunged my knife into his back.

Blood sprayed all over my chest.

"Dammit!" I was going to need to buy more soap before the week was out.

The wolf left out a half howl then dropped.

The sailors and merchants on the docks, a hardened lot, did not flee in terror. Instead, they politely stepped out of the way. Passengers debarking the ships and other common folks, however, screamed and ran. In the distance, I heard a constable's whistle.

I looked back in time to see Lionheart loping toward me. On the dock lay two dead wolves.

Lionheart's eyes, now fiery red, met mine.

With a nod, we raced after the others.

They ran ahead of us. At the end of the dock, there was a car waiting. Antoinette, Alodie's lead henchman, was waiting with one more of the Lolita girls. The Lolita girl who'd been on the ship pulled Cole toward the auto.

"Hell's bells, they have a getaway," I warned Lionheart.

Lionheart pushed past me, his speed startling me. He leaped once more, landing between them and the waiting auto.

Lionheart grabbed the Lolita by the throat. I could hear the werewolf's neck break under his grasp.

Seeing the fray underway, Antoinette emerged from the auto. She pulled her pistol and aimed at Lionheart.

"Richard," I called in warning.

I trained both my pistols on Antoinette and fired.

Lionheart turned, looking behind him.

My bullets hit Antoinette squarely in the chest. The

werewolf dropped. Cole moved away from the others but didn't shift form.

The other Lolita who'd come with Antoinette, seeing her partners fall as Lionheart and I cut our way through them, shifted into wolf form and fled.

I caught up to Lionheart. He grabbed Cole by the neck and leaned into the boy's face, staring him down. Lionheart's eyes flashed red. A low growl emanated from his chest.

Cyril's son looked from Lionheart, who had not stopped growling at him, to me. To my surprise, I saw fear in the boy's eyes.

He had not shifted form, had made no move to resist Lionheart. He didn't appear to be carrying any weapons. In fact, he'd done…nothing.

"Lionheart," I said.

The constable's whistles were growing louder, coming closer.

Lionheart's grip on the boy's throat squeezed tighter. He growled again.

"Lionheart."

The boy managed to get out a single word, "Sir."

"Richard, look at him. He's scared. He's not a threat. And we need to go," I said.

Lionheart studied the boy's face closer and breathed in deeply. Realizing I was right, he relaxed.

I watched in awe as the man I knew returned, the

wolfy features dissolving back into the handsome knight I'd grown accustomed to. Of course, now his clothes were tattered, but otherwise, he was once more the scholar I knew.

"Alodie's auto," I said, touching Lionheart's arm gently. "We need to leave before the constables show up. I'll keep an eye on him," I said, motioning to Cole.

Lionheart looked from my hand to my face, the shadow of the unfamiliar rage in his face slowly flickering out. He nodded.

Pulling my silver blade, I took Cole by the arm. "Don't try me," I told him.

The boy looked from the knife to me. "No, ma'am," he said then came along quietly. I pushed him into the auto, sliding in beside him.

Lionheart slipped behind the wheel and a moment later, we were rocketing through the streets of London back toward Temple Square.

As we drove, the boy's wide eyes took in the city. As we rounded Tinker's Tower, he frowned visibly.

"Never a more hated sight," he whispered then sat back in the seat, his expression dark. For the first time, I saw a flicker of red in his eyes.

I stared at him.

Dammit, Alodie. Just, dammit.

I leaned forward toward the driver's seat. "Richard," I whispered.

"Yes. I see," he replied but said nothing more.

I sat back and slipped my knife into my belt. I wasn't going to need it.

CHAPTER 19
Get the Message?

When we arrived at Temple Square, there was a flurry of activity.

Cole and I exited the auto and waited while Lionheart spoke to his knights.

"The Templars are honorable, not like the others," I whispered to Cole. "Tell them the truth about how you got here. They will believe you."

The boy looked down at me. He really did look like his father, except for his eyes. In Cole's eyes was a softness and sensitivity that had nothing to do with Cyril.

"Thank you, ma'am," he said. "I just… I just want to go home."

Lionheart rejoined me, pulling off his tattered shirt as he slipped on another.

My eyes lingered where they shouldn't have. From his chest to his stomach, he was a wall of muscle. But he was covered in scars. The knight's history was written on his flesh.

"Thank you, Agent Louvel," Lionheart said, motioning to two Templars to take Cole from my watch.

"Remember," I told the boy.

He inclined his head to me.

"And what should he remember?" Lionheart asked me.

"That the Templars are a force of good and that he should tell the truth."

"The truth being?"

"You saw for yourself. That boy is no alpha. Alodie was using him. He doesn't want to be here."

Lionheart nodded. "I concur. We'll question him."

"I need to go back to headquarters and address the mess at the dock," I said. "And you?"

"Alodie is still missing. I'll go with a band of knights and hunt her down. By morning, you may be in want of a job, Agent Louvel."

"Ah, but you forget something."

"And that is?"

"Someone still needs to keep an eye on you."

Lionheart chuckled. "Whatever would I do without you, Agent Louvel?"

"I'd hate to imagine."

A moment later, Sir Handel joined us. "Sir, a message," he told Lionheart.

Lionheart nodded to him, motioning for him to wait a moment.

The knight pressed the message toward Lionheart again. "Sir."

Lionheart took the note from Sir Handel's hand.

Taking my cue, I inclined my head to Lionheart. "Be careful, Sir Richard."

"You too, Agent Louvel," he replied.

I turned and headed out of Temple Square. I groaned inwardly when I thought about all the paperwork I was going to have to fill out regarding the incident at the docks. But first, I needed to check in with Edwin. Running around with Lionheart all night had my heart and mind twisted up. Seeing Edwin would set me back to right again. I was sure of it.

RM

WHEN I ARRIVED AT HEADQUARTERS, IT WAS LATE AT night. Stopping at dispatch, I asked for a few agents to be sent to the docks to clean up the mess and to hush the Bow Street Boys. With that done, I headed inside to see if Edwin was still there.

Annoying, distracting, and completely endearing, Lionheart's behavior confused me. He had a woman who loved him. But he didn't love her. What did that mean? Did it mean anything? I didn't know what to think. He cared enough about me to inquire with the Dís. What did *that* mean? Did Lionheart actually have genuine feelings for me?

Distracted by my thoughts, I didn't even notice that someone was sitting in my chair until I'd nearly stumbled upon her. Agent Rose was leaning back in my seat, her feet up on my desk. She was scanning through a file.

"Your wolves are making a mess in the dark district, Louvel. It's practically a bloodbath down there," she said, flipping through the pages.

"The Templars are cleaning up the streets tonight."

"That's all well and good for you, but damned if I didn't lose a mark in the process."

"Sorry," I said with a grin.

"Looking for Agent Hunter, I suppose," she said absently as she pushed a lock of her long, blonde hair over her shoulder.

"I was. How did you—"

"Come now, Agent. I've been around awhile. And you two skulking about the file room for a little snogging is not exactly covert."

I felt a blush rise to my cheeks. I was very glad that Agent Rose was not looking at me. "You're right. You do seem to be well-versed in soft, whispered tones between two people in love," I said, thinking back to the way Agent Rose and the vampire Constantine had spoken to one another.

Agent Rose paused as if she got my point. She looked at me over her shoulder, her blues eyes playful. "Something like that. Anyway, Agent Hunter isn't here. A runner came for him a bit ago with an urgent message. He looked a bit flustered. Never saw him like that before. He said he was going home."

A terrible feeling rocked my stomach. "Rose, do you have your auto?"

Sensing my alarm, she stood. "What is it?"

"Edwin's in trouble."

CHAPTER 20
Dirty Deeds

As Agent Rose's auto sped through the London streets, I felt like I couldn't breathe.

Alodie's threat of revenge repeated in my mind over and over again.

As Rose's auto slid to a stop outside Edwin's townhouse, my worst fears came to life as I saw the door had been bashed in and there was a pool of blood on the front steps.

From somewhere upstairs, I heard a gunshot.

I jumped out of the auto. Pulling both of my pistols, I raced toward the door.

"Louvel," Rose called behind me, cursing under her breath when I didn't stop.

Racing into the townhouse, I saw a very dead werewolf lying by the door. It was his blood that was dripping, thank God. The table in the foyer had been toppled over, the lamp broken. The scents of lamp oil and the musty odor of werewolves permeated the place.

There was another gunshot and the sound of commotion upstairs.

Rage rising up in me, I turned and raced up the stairs. A soft noise on the steps behind made me pause and look back. I was surprised to find Agent Rose there. How had she gotten there so quickly?

Upstairs, glass shattered, and I heard the sounds of fighting.

I raced up the steps in time to find Edwin cornered by three werewolves.

He was holding his own but clearly outnumbered.

Raising my pistol, I shot.

The first werewolf fell.

Agent Rose jumped onto the banister, and moving fast, she rushed another of the werewolves. Pulling the knives she always wore on her belt, she sliced as she leaped toward the werewolf.

There was a hissing sound as silver met flesh. The werewolf howled then fell.

Grabbing a silver candelabra off the table behind him, Edwin swiped the remaining werewolf across the face then kicked her toward me. Unsheathing my knife, I seized the Lolita and slid my blade along her throat, ending her sorry life. I dropped the werewolf and rushed to Edwin.

"Edwin," I said, eyeing him over. He was unhurt.

"Clemeny, thank god. I got a message you needed me to return home urgently."

"Should have taken me with you," Agent Rose said.

"I—I wasn't thinking straight. I could only think of —" Edwin began then looked at me.

"I'm all right," I reassured him then looked at the bodies lying on the floor. "Alodie. She told me we were going to pay for messing up her plans. Your servants?"

"In a safe room in the basement."

I nodded then looked over the bodies lying there. Alodie had sworn revenge on us. Tonight, her entire plan was unraveling. This was a desperate move, one last strike to take vengeance before it was too late. But it wasn't just Edwin and me on which she'd sworn revenge. She'd also promised to take revenge on Lionheart.

As I stood there, my mind went back to Temple Square and Sir Handel who'd been pressing an urgent message to Lionheart.

I gasped.

"Clemeny? What is it?" Edwin asked.

"Bryony. Oh my god, we need to hurry."

The three of us headed across town to Temple Square. When we arrived, I spotted Sir Handel at the gate.

"You there! Sir Handel."

"Agent Louvel?"

"Where is Lionheart?"

"He left right after you, Agent."

"The message you gave Lionheart. Who did it come from?"

"Sir Geoffrey."

Dammit! "Where did Sir Geoffrey take Bryony Paxton?"

"Miss Paxton?"

"Yes! Quickly man, your alpha is in trouble."

"They were headed to her flat in Chelsea then out to the Lionheart's country house," he said then pulled out a notepad. Jotting down both addresses, he handed a paper to me.

I rushed back to the car. "Chelsea," I told Agent Rose as I jumped back in. Rose pulled a lever on her auto. The vehicle shot down the street.

"Clemeny?" Edwin said.

"I just hope we aren't too late," I said, glancing out the window, a sharp pain rocking my stomach.

BITCHES AND BRAWLERS

AGENT ROSE SLOWED HER AUTO TO A STOP, PULLING UP behind the vehicle Lionheart and I had lifted from Antoinette. I glanced up at the windows of Bryony Paxton's townhouse. Everything was dark. Slipping my hand into my vest pocket, I pulled on my night optic.

The three of us slid out of the auto and headed up the steps to the townhouse. It was as silent as the grave inside and just as dark.

My heart was slamming hard in my chest, and a sick feeling rocked my stomach.

What if we were too late?

What if Bryony and Sir Richard were both already dead?

No. That couldn't happen.

Edwin pulled his pistol and slowly opened the door.

Activating the light on my optic, everything glowed green. My pistol in one hand, my dagger in the other, I entered the building.

Edwin and Agent Rose followed behind me. There were visible signs of a struggle. From broken glass, toppled furniture, to blood smeared on the wall, it was very evident a fight had gone down. As we neared the base of the stairs, I found the first body. From what was still recognizable of his mangled face, I knew him as a former member of the Whitechapel pack.

"Watch your—" I was about to say *step* but Agent Rose deftly worked her way around the body as if she saw it plain as day. I glanced at her, suppressing a surprised gasp when her eyes shimmered silver for the briefest of moments.

She met my gaze then winked at me.

What the hell?

Reaching out for Edwin, I gently guided him around the body then we headed up the steps.

I listened for signs of trouble.

There was nothing.

It was deadly silent.

We passed another body on the stairs.

On the second floor landing, we came across four more bodies.

Edwin paused at a side table and lit a lamp. We all stood and stared at the bloody scene.

At the end of the hallway, I heard a strange sound, like a muffled sob.

"Richard," I whispered, rushing to the end of the hall.

As I went, I spotted the body of Sir Geoffrey lying in the hallway.

Agent Rose and Edwin rushed after me.

When I got to the door, I stopped.

Again, I heard that strange sound.

Standing beside me, Agent Rose nodded to me then slowly opened the door. I pulled the hammer back on my pistol and stepped inside.

The light coming from Edwin's lamp cast a soft orange glow in the room, making long shadows out of our silhouettes.

The place was a bloodbath. There were wolf parts everywhere, blood on the floor, walls, and ceiling.

If it wasn't for the striking color of her blonde, nearly silver-colored hair, I wouldn't have recognized the heap of pulp that had once been Alodie. She had been beaten bloody and unrecognizable and was missing at least one limb. There were other bodies in the room, but there was no telling who they'd been.

At the center of the room, with Bryony's lifeless body lying at his feet, stood Lionheart.

Blood dripped from his fingers as he stood there shaking. He was covered in blood and bits. He stared at Bryony whose vacant blue eyes looked toward me, the lamplight reflecting dimly where life had once been. She was gone.

Lionheart's head was bent, shoulders slumped, his hands trembling.

"Clemeny," he whispered in a broken voice.

In that single moment, I couldn't breathe.

Agent Rose set her hand on my arm. "Agent Hunter and I will see to this," she said then leaned toward my ear. "Get him out of here."

I looked back at Edwin.

He had a strange, frozen expression on his face.

Holstering my gun, I went to Lionheart. He was splattered with blood, his mouth bloody, his clothes torn. There were bites on his exposed flesh.

"Come with me," I said, taking him by the arm. "They will take care of her."

Lionheart nodded.

Bending, I closed Bryony's eyes. Then taking the werewolf by the hand, I led Lionheart from the room.

As I passed Edwin, I couldn't—wouldn't—meet his eyes.

I didn't want him to see, didn't want him to guess.

Lionheart's hand in mine, I led him from the room and back out into the city. I scanned the streets. I needed to get him away from there. Immediately.

"When you're feeling better, you're going to owe me a huge thanks for making me drive this accursed thing," I said, settling him into Antoinette's auto. I slid into the driver's seat. I had hoped the joke would reach him, but there was no expression on Lionheart's face.

"It's all right, Richard," I said, taking his hand in mine. "I've got you."

Starting the auto, I turned and headed back across town toward Temple Square.

CHAPTER 21
Reckonings

When I arrived at Temple Square, everything was in upheaval. They let me through the gate. I drove in, parking the auto.

Lionheart got out and headed directly to the chapel.

Sir Blackwood, who looked like his night hadn't been much better than mine, crossed the square to me.

"Agent Louvel?" Sir Blackwood said, looking from Lionheart to me.

I shook my head. "Alodie is finished. But... Bryony Paxton was murdered. I'm sorry, but Sir Geoffrey also did not survive. The Red Capes are on site."

Agent Blackwood frowned. "I see. Maybe I should..." he said then turned toward the chapel. He paused and looked back at me. "You go. I will see to the rest of it."

I inclined my head to him then went to Temple Church. I entered quietly, holding the door behind me so it would merely click shut. Lionheart was leaning over the pedestal of holy water. He'd washed his hands and face. Streaks of orange-tinted water dripped from his hands into the bowl. His tattered shirt lay on the ground.

Moving carefully, I stepped toward him.

I watched as he inhaled deeply. He looked up at me from below a lock of hair. Turning, he advanced on me with such fierceness that I was struck dumb. He crossed the room, grabbed me by the waist, and placed such a fierce kiss on my lips that I was too shocked to think.

But not too shocked to fall into the embrace I had so desperately been trying to avoid, the kiss I had wanted and wanted to escape at all costs. I closed my eyes and kissed Richard Spencer, the man, not the wolf. The man whom my heart yearned for, but whom I knew I had to deny.

I felt his hot tears on my cheeks as he pressed me closer and closer. I fell into his embrace until I saw stars before my eyes and felt dizzy.

After a time, Lionheart pulled back and stared at me.

I reached out and touched his cheek, wiping the tears from his face.

The muscles around his eyes twitched and then those around his mouth.

"Clemeny," he whispered, touching my face. "I...I..."

Turning from me, he walked across the chapel to the altar, falling on his knees before the effigy of Christ hanging there.

"God, why have you cursed me? Why have you made me into this? Why have you done this to me? I was loyal to you, and you took everything from me. I can have nothing. No one. Why, God, why?" Lionheart shouted angrily.

Aghast, I stood there, not knowing what to do.

Lionheart moaned softly.

Knees shaking, I stepped toward him.

"Clemeny, please. Please go. I'm sorry. Clemeny, please. Please go," he whispered.

I stared at him.

Without knowing what better course to take, I turned and left the chapel, the square, the city. Walking blindly, I made my way back across the river, my mind turning in a fit of confusion. It wasn't until I'd slipped into my window at Missus Coleridge's that I finally shook myself out of my dazed state. Exhausted and confused, I sat down on the floor, pulling my knees to my chest, and closed my eyes.

"Bryony," I whispered, remembering her lifeless blue eyes. "I'm sorry."

CHAPTER 22
Red Roses

I must have fallen asleep because I woke late the next day when someone knocked on my door.

I swallowed the anxious feeling inside me, dreading who might be on the other side of the door. If it was Edwin, I owed him an explanation. If it was Lionheart, I wasn't ready. If it was Missus Coleridge, I was in no mood.

"Yes?" I called.

"It's Sir Blackwood."

I opened the door to find the Templar knight standing there. He handed me a package.

"What's this?" I asked.

"From Sir Richard."

"How is—"

"He left on an airship this morning. He's taking Cole

back to America, and then he plans to return to the Holy Land for a time thereafter."

I stared at the werewolf.

"I suspect things will be quiet now, Agent Louvel. But I am available if there is a need. Until Lionheart returns, of course."

"Very well."

Sir Blackwood nodded then paused. "There is something else for you. Outside. With Lionheart's compliments. I... I already discussed it with your landlady," he said then coughed politely. "Very well," he said, bowing briefly, then he left.

Closing and locking the door behind him, I opened the parcel. Inside, I found a piece of paper with an address in London, written in Lionheart's elegant hand, and a key. Nothing more.

No note.

No words of explanation.

No nothing, just an address and a key.

I frowned. What did I expect? Hell, I didn't even know what I was thinking, feeling. Why did I expect Lionheart to know any better than me?

I set the package down. Working quickly, I cleaned myself up and redressed. I would need to go to headquarters and file about a million pieces of paperwork—and face Edwin—soon, but not yet.

Moving as quietly as possible, I headed downstairs

to find Missus Coleridge waiting for me at the bottom of the steps.

"Clemeny," she said, her eyes shining with excitement. "Was that your gentleman? Oh, a fine cut of a man. Not talkative though. Come look," she said then pushed open the front door. I followed her outside to find Lionheart's steamcycle sitting there.

"Noisy machines, but at least you won't have to walk everywhere anymore, eh Clemeny?"

"It's on loan from a friend," I said.

"The handsome friend?"

"A different handsome friend."

"Oh, my. I'll need to start advertising your room soon," Missus Coleridge said with a laugh.

I clapped her on the shoulder then went to the steamcycle. Of all means of conveyance that weren't my feet, the steamcycle rattled my stomach the least. And Missus Coleridge was right, chasing wolves by foot was getting old. Lionheart would have a hard time getting the cycle back from me when he returned. If he returned. I stared at the bike. But Lionheart already knew that, knew that I needed something. That's why he'd sent the bike to me.

Noting the address written on the paper once more, I stashed the note and key in my pocket, pulled on a pair of goggles, and climbed on. Switching on the machine, I gave Missus Coleridge a wave.

"Be careful," she called.

I grinned at her. If she only knew. I turned the bike and headed back into the city. As I wound down the narrow London streets, I moved with the machine. Feeling the wind on my face and controlling the movement of the cycle made my stomach ease. Perhaps I could get used to this after all.

Making my way through the city, I drove to a small neighborhood not far from the Tower of London. The address Lionheart had given me directed me to a narrow street. I drove slowly, noting how the buildings narrowed to form a bottleneck, which opened up into a cul-de-sac. From the look of the buildings, I could tell this was a very old part of London. But it was well-kept. I parked the machine at a gate at the address on the paper and switched it off. I looked at the building. The other structures appeared to have been built up all around it. Slipping off my goggles, I went to the wrought-iron gate which was locked. I was no expert on architecture, but this place had to date back at least to the medieval period. On the other side of the gate was a narrow passage that led into a green space on the other side.

"Hello?" I called.

A door inside the passage opened, and a very bent old woman with white hair appeared.

"Oh," she said, clasping her hands together when

she saw me. "Here you are. Come along, dear. Miss Louvel, isn't it?" she asked, opening the gate for me.

"Um. Yes."

"Good, good. Professor Spencer said to expect you," she said. "Your key will unlock the gate as well. Just go ahead and use that next time. We have everything cleaned up and prepared for you. This way," she said then motioned for me to follow her.

She led me through the narrow passage under the building. The low, arched gateway exited on the other side into a small courtyard. Much to my surprise, a small building was sitting there, a garden, including an apple tree, in front of the house. The garden was full of flowers and statues. In one corner, I noticed a stone structure that looked a bit like a cave. It was shell-shaped and made of stone. Years and years of candles had dripped wax down the cave walls. A statue of a woman sat on a pedestal at the center. All around the space was an ancient looking stone wall.

"What is this place?" I asked.

"Are you a scholar like the professor? As I explained to Professor Spencer, Saint Joan's cathedral was torn down long ago, but the rectory and grotto remain. Of course, the grotto dates before Saint Joan's time. It was built right near the Roman wall. Of course, you probably know that already. The grotto—that's what Professor Spencer was interested in, the Roman connection. I believe he said the grotto used to be part of the Roman Temple of Vesta. I never knew that part. Holy ground, that's what Professor Spencer called this place. You have your key?"

I stuck my hand into my vest and pulled out the key Lionheart had left me.

"Very good. Now, I already employed a maid for you. She will start next week. Go in and have a look around. My place is just off the passageway inside the gate. Knock if you need anything. I'm so glad to see that someone will be using the house again. I was afraid it was going to be torn down. Welcome to your new home, Miss Louvel," the old woman said then turned and left.

With a shaking hand, I went to the door.

Was this real?

I unlocked the door and pushed it open. "Hello?"

My voice echoed throughout the space.

I entered slowly.

There was a tick of a grandfather clock somewhere inside the house. The place smelled of wood polish and soap. Everything sparkled. The furniture was dated but nice. The floors and walls were all made of hardwood which had been finely polished. Oil paintings of pastoral scenes adorned the walls. The lamps had been converted to gas. The first floor consisted of a cozy parlor, a small dining room, a kitchen, butler's pantry, and a library. I wandered up to the second floor where I found two bedrooms. The first bedroom was primly decorated, lavender sprigs on the wallpaper. There were paintings of the French countryside hanging on the walls. That room, apparently, was meant for Grand-mère. I entered the second bedroom to find it mostly empty save a bed and a massive old wardrobe. The wardrobe's door was slightly ajar.

I crossed the room and opened it. When I did so, an entire hamper of bright red rose petals cascaded down on me. I was engulfed by their heavenly perfume. After they had washed over me, dusting the floor all around me, I looked back at the wardrobe and found a beautiful red gown hanging there.

Taking the fabric in my hand, my fingers slid across the silk. I closed my eyes, a wash of emotions crashing over me.

Lionheart had found me a house.

On holy ground.

He wanted to keep me safe.

He wanted to keep me safe where he had failed his wife…and now Bryony.

He must have picked up the place after that day at Missus Coleridge's. That meant whatever feelings Lionheart had for me, whatever intentions he had, were born long before that kiss. I remembered Lionheart's words in the chapel, the pain in his voice.

Closing my eyes, I inhaled deeply, breathing in the rosy scent.

What in the hell was I supposed to do now?

I went to the window and looked out on the little square.

Sunlight streamed into the garden, casting a cheerful glow on the flowers growing there. I imagined my grand-mère in this pretty place, happily attending to the flowers. She would love it here. And she would be safe here. What happened with Fenton wouldn't happen again.

"Okay, Lionheart," I said to the absent werewolf. "I'll take it, but that doesn't make me yours."

If that's even what he wanted.

God knows I had no idea what he wanted.

I closed my eyes, remembering Bryony once more. Lionheart had gone back to the holy land. He was trying to find himself and his way back to God. I knew he would feel responsible for Bryony's death, that it would weigh on him. There was nothing I could do to lift his burden, but I shared it. If I had stopped Alodie earlier, Bryony would still be alive.

I squeezed the key in my hand.

I really needed to go back to headquarters, to talk to Edwin, to explain everything. But what was I going to say? I hardly understood myself. With Alodie gone, I was down one problem. But now? I shook my head.

Until I knew what to say to Edwin, maybe I had no business saying anything at all. Or maybe that was just me running scared. But of what? The one thing I wanted most? To love and be loved by someone who could love me back.

Slipping my key back into my pocket, I headed back outside. Locking up the house behind me, I went to the steamcycle and slipped on. The engine started with a hiss. I pulled away from the little house and headed away from London to the one place where I knew I could find good advice.

CHAPTER 23
Horizons

"Agent Louvel? I'm sorry, Mrs. Briarwood is out, but Agent Briarwood is in the garden. Shall I let him know you're here?"

"Please."

Motioning for me to come inside, I entered Jessica and Quinn's sunny little house and waited for the footman to announce me. The foyer was painted a lively yellow color, and the walls were covered with colorful paintings of flowers created by Jessica herself. She had a deft hand. Her oil paintings were rich and bright.

"Clem?" Quinn called from the back of the house.

Grinning, I followed the sound of his voice, passing the footman along the way.

I found Quinn in the garden, leaning against his cane as he looked me over from head to toe, concern on his face. He motioned for me to come then closed the glass door behind me. "Jessica is out. She was invited to tea."

"You didn't want to go and chat with the husbands?"

Quinn laughed gruffly. "No, thank you."

I smirked at him then went to the easel sitting in the garden. On it, I found a painting in progress. Jessica was painting the bright pink, orange, and purple tulips growing in the flowerbed. "Pretty," I said.

"You should see the nursery. She's painting a mosaic."

I smiled and nodded.

"So, what happened?" Quinn asked.

"Nothing much."

"Come on, Clem. I've known you too long," Quinn said, slowly lowering himself back into his seat. "Something happened."

Sighing, I flopped into a white wicker chaise. "Alodie is dead."

Quinn nodded stoically. I could sense his mixed feelings, but he didn't say anything. "Was I right about Cyril's boy?"

"Yes and no. It was Alodie's plan to crown him. But he didn't want to be here, got sucked into Alodie's game."

"Then he's lucky to be alive. Who took out Alodie?"

"Lionheart. Alodie went after Bryony Paxton. Lionheart didn't get there in time. Alodie paid dearly," I said, remembering the pulpy mess that had once been the she-wolf. Her body had been broken almost beyond recognition. I remembered the blood on Lionheart's face. I shook my head.

Quinn sighed. "I'm sorry to hear about Bryony. Her quick thinking saved my life. It's a terrible loss."

"Yes."

"The Templars have the city under control now? Fully?"

"Yes."

"Then why are you here? What happened?"

I sighed. "Lionheart."

Quinn grunted, but he didn't sound entirely surprised.

Neither of us said anything for a long time.

Finally, Quinn said, "Edwin Hunter is a good match for you, Clemeny."

"I know."

"And I think you care for him."

"I do."

Quinn tapped his cane. "I remember when you and I first went around to see Lionheart. That old werewolf would barely speak two words to me, but when he saw you, something in him woke up."

"He's very awake now."

Quinn sighed. "He cannot be trusted. He isn't like us."

Like us. "He was. Once."

"Once, but not anymore. Don't make the same mistake I made with Alodie. I felt sorry for her, sympathy for her plight. I forgot that we are not the same. It nearly cost me my life."

Reaching inside my vest, I pulled out the paper Lionheart had given me at the pub. I handed it to Quinn.

"Evelyn DuLac," he read then wagged the paper in the air a moment. "Why do I know this name?"

"She's a druid."

"A druid. That's right. Why do you have her name, Clem?"

"What if… What if I'm like them?"

"What do you mean?"

"You know what I mean."

Quinn frowned. "No."

"No what?"

"Whatever you're thinking, no. You aren't one of them."

"But there is something different about me."

"You're smart, strong, and perceptive, and you have a powerful sixth sense, but that doesn't make you one of them. At least, not in the same way. The lupine affliction, the vampiric seed, and all the rest…it changes the victim. Maybe they were once human, but they aren't anymore. Even if you are *gifted*, you aren't preternatural," he handed the paper back to me. "Are you going?"

I shrugged. "I don't know. I need to settle things here first."

"Then settle things. I take it this business with Lionheart made a mess of things between you and Edwin."

"I'm not sure. I don't know what Edwin's thinking. Hell, I don't even know what I'm thinking."

"Edwin is a good man. You deserve a good *man*."

Not werewolf. Quinn was right. Whatever was trying to bloom between Lionheart and me shouldn't come to life. It wasn't good for anyone. Not for Lionheart. Not for me.

I rose. "Thanks, Quinn."

He nodded. "If you decide to go to Cornwall and you need your partner, I'm always here for you."

I leaned in and kissed him on the forehead. "Thanks."

"Want a drink before you go?"

I shook my head. "Lionheart left me his steamcycle. He... He's gone to the Holy Land for a bit. I don't want to wreck the thing."

"Holy Land? Well, that ought to put him back to right. All right, partner. All right. Be safe out there."

"Thank you."

"And make good choices."

"Of course."

"And don't fall in love with a bloody werewolf."

I chuckled, squeezed Quinn's hand, then turned and headed out of the house.

Sliding back on the cycle, I pulled on my goggles. Quinn once told me that one day I was going to want something different, one day I was going to want a peaceful life. At the time, the idea seemed ridiculous. With Edwin in my life, however, my opinion had started to change. I'd just spotted the edge of that life on my horizon. There was only one person who had a place in a future like that. And he wasn't a werewolf. I clicked the bike on and pulled out, heading back toward London, headquarters, and Edwin.

CONTINUE CLEMENY'S ADVENTURES IN *HOWLS AND HALLOWS*

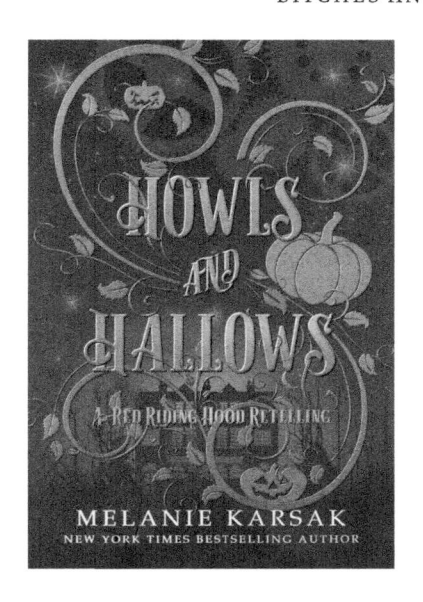

HOWLS AND HALLOWS

A Red Riding Hood Retelling

MELANIE KARSAK
NEW YORK TIMES BESTSELLING AUTHOR

About the Author

New York Times and *USA Today* bestselling author Melanie Karsak is the author of *The Celtic Blood Series, The Road to Valhalla Series, The Celtic Rebels Series, Steampunk Fairy Tales* and many more works of fiction. The author currently lives in Florida with her husband and two children.

- amazon.com/author/melaniekarsak
- facebook.com/authormelaniekarsak
- instagram.com/karsakmelanie
- pinterest.com/melaniekarsak
- bookbub.com/authors/melanie-karsak
- youtube.com/@authormelaniekarsak

Also by Melanie Karsak

THE CELTIC BLOOD SERIES:

Highland Raven

Highland Blood

Highland Vengeance

Highland Queen

THE CELTIC REBELS SERIES:

Queen of Oak: A Novel of Boudica

Queen of Stone: A Novel of Boudica

Queen of Ash and Iron: A Novel of Boudica

THE ROAD TO VALHALLA SERIES:

Under the Strawberry Moon

Shield-Maiden: Under the Howling Moon

Shield-Maiden: Under the Hunter's Moon

Shield-Maiden: Under the Thunder Moon

Shield-Maiden: Under the Blood Moon

Shield-Maiden: Under the Dark Moon

THE SHADOWS OF VALHALLA SERIES:

Shield-Maiden: Winternights Gambit

Shield-Maiden: Gambit of Blood

Shield-Maiden: Gambit of Shadows

Shield-Maiden: Gambit of Swords

Eagles and Crows

The Blackthorn Queen

The Crow Queen

THE HARVESTING SERIES:

The Harvesting

Midway

The Shadow Aspect

Witch Wood

The Torn World

STEAMPUNK FAIRY TALES:

Curiouser and Curiouser: Steampunk Alice in Wonderland

Ice and Embers: Steampunk Snow Queen

Beauty and Beastly: Steampunk Beauty and the Beast

Golden Braids and Dragon Blades: Steampunk Rapunzel

THE RED CAPE SOCIETY

Wolves and Daggers

Alphas and Airships

Peppermint and Pentacles

Bitches and Brawlers

Howls and Hallows

Lycans and Legends

THE AIRSHIP RACING CHRONICLES:

Chasing the Star Garden

Chasing the Green Fairy

Chasing Christmas Past

THE CHANCELLOR FAIRY TALES:

The Glass Mermaid

The Cupcake Witch

The Fairy Godfather

The Vintage Medium

The Book Witch

                Find these books and more on Amazon!

Printed in Great Britain
by Amazon